Romance Unbound Publishing

Presents

Enslaved

by
Claire Thompson

Edited by Jae Ashley

Cover Design by Kelly Shorten

Print ISBN 978-1466421295

Copyright 2011 Claire Thompson
All rights reserved

Chapter 1

"That fucking little cunt."

Sam Ryker narrowed his eyes as he stared at the numbers on the computer screen and back again at the statement the banker had just faxed to him. Cold fury snaked its way through him, nearly obscuring the heat of a deeper hurt beneath it.

He closed his eyes, seizing the anger roiling within his brain in a mental fist and forcing it under control. Swiveling toward the window of the tiny office, he stared, unseeing, at the Manhattan skyline.

Maybe he was jumping to conclusions without having all the facts. Could it be a simple matter of a mistake in the numbers? Or did she have an explanation for the ten percent difference in what she claimed the bank charged for his two million dollar line of credit, a line that had been fully extended for the past eight months since she'd arranged it for him?

He'd brought Rae Johansen onboard to handle the financial side of his fledgling software company so he could focus on the product and the customers. He'd paid her when he couldn't pay himself, using every bit of his savings, relying on her, trusting her. They'd worked well together. She'd freed him from the annoying day-to-day details so he could focus on the core business. She'd had his back, or so he'd thought.

I would have found a way to help you, Rae. If you'd told me you needed it...

But life rarely worked out that way, did it? He would have given her his heart too, but she wasn't interested. The first time he'd laid eyes on her, he'd wanted her. Maybe that was his first mistake — letting his cock get in the way of his brain.

Sam closed his eyes, letting the image of Rae lying naked on his sheets flow into his mind. Those cobalt blue eyes flecked with bronze, the dark hair in a tumble around her face, the curve of her breast, the rope on her slender wrists binding her to the headboard as he loomed over her, plunging his cock into the soft, tight heat of her wet cunt...

He'd misjudged her desires, her readiness to submit. Or, more accurately, he'd judged her desire correctly — she wanted what he offered. She *needed* it. He could see it in the hunger in her eyes, the clench of her fingers and gasp of her breath — but she'd been scared. Scared not so much of him or what he offered, but of her own reaction to it. His mistake had been that he'd moved too fast. He'd wanted her too much and he'd paid the price.

Sam Ryker wasn't the type of man to go where he wasn't welcome. When she'd pulled back, he'd let her go. At the time, he'd told himself it was probably for the best. Everyone knew you shouldn't mix work with pleasure. Though it took a few weeks to work through the awkwardness on both sides, they'd managed to move on. They were both professional enough not to let their brief fling interfere with things.

If he still dreamed of her at night, his cock fisted in his hand, images of her naked and at his mercy streaming through his mind, it was forgotten by morning. The complex and absorbing programming code and the daily challenge of growing his business were more than enough distraction. A relationship would have only complicated matters. It was better this way.

Liar.

He returned his attention to the computer monitor, still struggling to come to terms with the evidence that stared him in the face. Yeah, he got it that she hadn't wanted to explore the Pandora's box of her own submissive sexuality when that particular lid was lifted, but he never dreamed she would take advantage of the trust he'd placed in her professionally.

If Rae were anyone else, he wouldn't have hesitated to call the police and have her arrested on the spot. But she wasn't anyone else. Even though it had been just the one time, Rae had left a part of herself like a shard of glass lodged painfully in his heart, despite the scar tissue of time that covered it. What he still wouldn't give to have her in his bed again, or on her knees at his feet, looking up at him with those luminous dark blue eyes…

"She needs to be taught a lesson," he said softly, as a delicious and dangerous idea edged its way into his head. "She needs to be punished."

Sam glanced at his watch. It was only seven-thirty in the morning. Too bad. What he had to say couldn't wait. He hit the speed dial on his BlackBerry and lifted it to his ear.

"Hey, Sam." Her voice, low and husky, stroked his senses as it always did, like fingers playing over his skin. Her tone was relaxed and easy. She had no idea she'd been busted.

"There's something I need to discuss with you."

"Sure. What's up?"

"No. In person. When can you get here?"

"Hey, I've barely had my coffee. Can it wait until later in the day? Want to send me an email with the details? What do you need? If it's about the quarterly tax payment, I've already got—"

"No," Sam interrupted. "It can't wait. I want you here. Now."

"What's the topic?" she pressed. "That way I can prepare—"

"We'll discuss it when you get here."

There was a pause and Sam could almost feel her frown through the phone. She didn't like it when he pulled rank. Or maybe she understood from his tone all was not well in paradise. Tough shit. He waited.

Finally she said, "Okay, Sam. I can be there in an hour. That work for you?"

"Like a charm."

~*~

Rae opened her compact and checked her face in the tiny mirror as the subway hurtled beneath the city toward Sam's building. Who did Sam think he was, ordering her to drop everything and head across town like his personal lackey? It was bad enough she had to work from home — his broom closet of an office might be at a prestigious Manhattan address, but it barely had room for his desk and three computers, much less another person. He paid her a decent salary, but still hadn't come through with his promise to give her a stake in the company, even though they nearly had the *Ichi* deal in their pockets. Well, in *his* pocket.

Here he was, poised to earn tens of millions on the software deal with a prime Japanese company and he still put her off with vague promises. "I should never have slept with him," she chided herself for the hundredth time. "It made him take me less seriously as a business partner."

What a perv he'd turned out to be, into all that whips and chains crap! The bondage thing *had* been kind of exciting, if she were honest, but she wasn't that kind of woman. No man told her what to do, not in the bedroom or out of it. No, it was better she'd nipped their personal relationship in the bud before things got out of hand.

Especially with what she'd been doing with the books.

She hated herself for it, but she hadn't seen any other way out. Not without admitting she'd fucked up big time. She only needed a little more to finally extricate herself from that hideous, money-draining, loser real estate deal she'd let herself be talked into. She should have known it was too good to be true. She'd committed the cardinal sin in business — she'd let her greed get the better of her.

So far her arrangement had gone without a hitch and she was nearly home free. As soon as she could get the debt paid and the back taxes she owed taken care of, she'd never do anything like this again. She'd stay on the straight and narrow, and give her all to *Ryker Solutions*. She'd make it up to Sam by working her ass off. Maybe then he'd finally make her partner like he promised.

I want you here. Now.

He'd sounded pissed. Rae hugged herself as his words played back in her mind. He'd never summarily ordered her to drop everything and get her ass to the office like that before. Was he on to her? Was she going to get busted this close to the end? She shook away the thought.

Rae pushed through the crowded subway station and up the stairs to the street, where the heat hit her with a humid blast. She hurried down the block toward Sam's office building and through the revolving doors.

Sam was too clueless when it came to finances. When he'd hired her he hadn't even set up the company properly and was paying way too much in fees and taxes. He was one of those typical geeks who was brilliant at programming but could barely remember to pay his own bills. She'd spent months getting that side of his business straightened out and procuring the line of credit he needed for it to really take off.

He needed her. Without her, he would never have gotten the *Ichi* deal. Reminding herself of this, she smiled bravely at her image in the mirrored elevator door and squared her shoulders as it opened. With a determined stride, she moved down the hallway, the very picture of feminine competence.

With a perfunctory knock, she pushed open the door of *Ryker Solutions*. "I made it," she announced, dropping her briefcase on one of the chairs in front of Sam's desk and settling herself into the other. "Now, what's so urgent it couldn't be handled on the phone?"

Sam, who had been typing something on his keyboard, looked up slowly. In spite of her nervous anticipation, she felt her body react as he swept her with a fiery gaze. There was a kind of power in his face that she responded to on a gut level, even though intellectually she rejected it. It was that power, that easy arrogance, that had made her tumble into bed with him in the first place. It was that same power that had scared her and made her reject him out of hand.

Fortunately she was wearing one of her Xena Warrior bras, the kind with enough padding to hide her perking nipples. Ignoring the sudden warmth between her legs, she smoothed her face into a bland, inquiring smile and waited.

"What's the interest rate on my line of credit?" Sam's blue-grey eyes looked steely as he pinned her with his look.

Rae's stomach gave an unpleasant lurch and she felt the pulse in her neck quicken. She kept her bland smile and pretended to think for a second. "Eighteen, but I've been working on getting you a lower rate. Now that the company's got more of a track record – "

"Try again."

"I'm sorry?" Rae's heart was beating too fast. She felt almost faint.

"Not as sorry as you're going to be, little girl."

"Now, just a minute, nobody talks – "

"Save it, Rae. I'm onto you. Jerry Mitchell clued me in."

"I have no idea what you're talking about," she lied. Her mind was skittering like a rat tossed on the deck of a sinking ship. Desperately she tried to think, to come up with an excuse, but all she managed was, "Who's Jerry Mitchell?"

"He's a senior VP over at the bank. I happened to run into him at the golf course yesterday. He asked about the business, just shooting the breeze. He was surprised to hear I was paying such a high rate. Said he'd look into it for me come Monday. Called me this morning and said I was mistaken. Said the rate's *eight* percent, not eighteen."

Sam turned the monitor so Rae could see her own numbers, the false numbers she kept in case Sam had ever bothered to check. He pushed what looked like a bank statement across the desk toward her.

She opened her mouth to deny it, to protest, to make up a story, but no words came. She tried to swallow but her throat felt as if it were filled with rocks. He was watching her with a cold expression.

"There must be a mistake…" she finally managed to whisper.

He ignored this. "You owe me over a hundred thousand dollars. I'll expect it by five o'clock this afternoon."

Rae gripped her chair. This was insane. "I can't—I didn't…"

He stood, towering over her. "Don't bother with your lies. It's here in black and white. You're busted. Get me the money or I call the cops."

"Sam, please," Rae said desperately. "Listen, I can explain."

Sam glared at her a moment longer but then, thank god, he sat down. "Okay. I'm listening. Make it good."

Rae closed her eyes, trying to compose herself. Did she tell him the truth? Would it make any difference? Aware she sounded defensive, she said, "You'd promised to give me a share in the company, in the profits. It's been months since you promised. I've done really good work for you, Sam. I've busted my ass to get this company good credit and new customers—"

"By robbing me blind? You have rather peculiar ideas of how to manage a company's finances." His voice was low, even menacing. She almost wished he'd yell instead, anything to this cold, hard way he was speaking. It chilled her to the bone.

"Talk to me, Rae. Tell me the truth."

The *or else* was implicit in his words. Frightened, Rae admitted, "I—I got into some financial trouble. With a real estate deal I became involved with. It went sour and my business partner left me holding the bag. I've been trying like hell to get out of debt and move on. I was just—just borrowing the funds for a while, till I could get back on my feet."

Sam steepled his fingers beneath his chin and leaned toward her, his eyes sparking. "So let me get this straight. You made a bad business deal and then decided to steal from me to get out of it? It never occurred to you to maybe come to me and ask for help? Or take out a legitimate loan somewhere? What the fuck, Rae? I trusted you."

The hardness in his tone was edged with hurt. Could it be he still cared for her on some level? Could she exploit that now to her advantage? Feeling like a shit for doing it, but also feeling pretty desperate in the circumstances, Rae allowed the very real tears pressing at her eyelids to escape and slip down her cheeks. She let the tremble she'd been holding at bay enter her voice and pouted, opening her eyes wide to make herself look as vulnerable as possible.

"Please, Sam," she said softly. "I'm so, so sorry. It was stupid. I was scared and in a jam and afraid to let you know how bad I'd fucked up. I'll do anything you want. *Anything.*" She put her hand on her throat and let it trail down her chest, drawing his eye to her breasts, now wishing she'd worn something sexy, instead of her no-nonsense blouse and suit jacket.

"Please," she whispered throatily. "I don't have the cash to repay you. Let me make this right some other way." She crossed her legs, causing her skirt to ride up higher on her thighs as she cast him a beseeching look.

A smile edged its way over Sam's lips and he narrowed his eyes. "Anything, huh," he drawled slowly. "Anything to avoid the certain jail time for embezzlement? Anything I want?"

"Anything," she affirmed, not liking his tone but not daring to show it.

He leaned back in his chair and put his hands behind his head, his smile almost friendly. "What makes you think you have something I want? Something worth that kind of money? Hmm?" His gaze was positively insolent as he undressed her with his eyes. Rae felt her face heat and she looked down. She had asked for this and she knew it.

"I asked you a question," the bastard persisted. "What have you got that I might want?"

She forced herself to look at him again, anger giving her courage. "You tell me," she said, trying to keep her voice even.

He stared at her a while, saying nothing. She tried not to fidget or scream. Finally he spoke, his voice low and calm, a small, almost cruel smile curving his lips. "Thirty days. You will give me thirty days."

Rae was confused. "What? Thirty days of what?"

"You'll spend thirty days in my dungeon, meditating on your crime and showing me just how very sorry you are. You'll be my sex slave. My toy to do with as I will. You'll serve your time, if you want to look at it that way, naked and chained."

Rae stared at him in utter disbelief, trying to process his insane and outrageous proposal. She forced herself to think, to try to make sense of what he was saying. He couldn't really be serious.

He was watching her, waiting for a response.

"You're joking," she finally managed. "Look, I can come up with the cash. Just give me some time—"

"Oh, you will, don't worry. One way or the other, you'll pay back every cent. But this deal is in addition to restitution. It's so you can avoid jail time and financial ruin. It's your punishment for being a very, very bad girl." His cold smile sent a shiver up Rae's spine.

The words burst from her lips before she could stop them. "What the fuck, Sam? A dungeon? Punishment? You can't be serious. This isn't the Dark Ages. This is

New York, not Tehran. You can't just tie a woman up and give her thirty lashes, for god's sake!"

"Sure I can. And I'll have fun doing it. You will be punished as I see fit. At the end of your penance period, we can decide where we go from there."

"How do I know there's an end to this, uh," she paused, but forced herself to say the word, "punishment? How can I trust you to keep your word? What's to stop you from blackmailing me for the rest of your life?"

Sam shook his head, his smile ironic. "Trust," he said in a musing tone. "Are you actually talking to me about trust? I'd say you don't have a whole hell of a lot of choice here. Take it or leave it."

He gazed at her, an implacable expression on his face. How had she ever been so stupid to think she could get away with her scam? Why hadn't she gone to him or somehow come up with the money she needed without resorting to theft? Why did she always take the easy way out when things got tough? Rae began to cry, dropping her head into her hands.

"Spare me the tears. You take what's due, Rae, you do the thirty days. Then we'll work out a repayment schedule. If you stick to the terms, then I won't call in the authorities. To give you some assurance, we'll write up an agreement that suits us both regarding the money you owe and my statement that it was money *lent*, not stolen."

She continued to cry, but she was listening, still trying to decide if he was really serious and if it was something she could do. Thirty days as someone's sex slave! The idea was preposterous, absurd, insane! And yet...and yet she couldn't deny the tiniest spark of excitement at the idea.

The thought of being kept naked and in chains in Sam Ryker's dungeon. His *dungeon*! What the hell did that even mean? Was it some dank, dark place with manacles on the walls like in a medieval castle? Or was it like those BDSM clubs she'd seen pictures of on the internet, with black walls and people dressed in leather with masks covering their faces and cat o' nine tails in their hands?

"Rae, look at me," Sam commanded.

Rae lifted her head slowly, focusing on Sam's face. "I need an answer. Do you agree to my terms or do I call the police? It's up to you." She stared at him, her mouth working, no sound issuing. Again she felt that raw power emanating from him, more than his usual casual arrogance and confidence. This felt different and, in spite of herself, Rae felt a tug of attraction.

Thirty days under lock and key, could she handle that? Could she trust him to stick to the terms? Did she have a choice? He held all the cards—there was nothing to negotiate.

Nevertheless, she clung to what he'd said earlier. "If I agree," she said slowly, "we'll sign that indemnifying agreement first, right? Before I go to your, uh, dungeon." The last word came out as a whisper.

Sam actually laughed. "You sound like an attorney. You'll get your agreement, don't worry—but when I say so, not you. We'll draw it up now and sign when the month is up."

He really was serious. It was finally sinking in. He meant it. He was going to hold her hostage for a month! "When—" Her voice came out as a croak. She cleared her throat and tried again. "When would this, uh, penance, start?"

"Now. You'll be going home with me."

"Now?" Rae squeaked. "I can't just up and leave things. I have food in my refrigerator that would rot. And I have other responsibilities. I'm still working on the *Ichi* deal. Don't you want that wrapped up?"

"We'll go together to your place and do what needs to be done to secure things until your return. The *Ichi* deal is pretty much in the bag at this point and anyway, it's not like you won't be around to consult if I need anything. I might let you out of the dungeon from time to time, if you're a very good girl."

"Sam, you can't..." Rae trailed off. Her heart was thumping loud in her ears and she felt dizzy and sick to her stomach.

"Oh, no? Watch me."

Chapter 2

"Take off your shoes."

They stood in the front hall of his home. Rae looked up at him with those big doe eyes and bit her lip, but she stepped out of her heels like a good girl.

"Unbutton your blouse."

He watched her swallow hard. She started to speak but he stopped her with a finger to her lips. "No. Remember, not a word."

He'd outlined the rules as he'd driven her from her place to his home in Brooklyn Heights, making them up as he went along. "While you're my sex slave, you won't speak unless spoken to. You will always answer any questions directly and honestly." He snorted, adding, "At least as honestly as you're capable of."

She opened her mouth as if to retort but, wisely, held her tongue. He continued. "You will obey whatever I ask of you to the letter, doing no more and no less than I demand. If you feel you have to say something to me, you will ask first for permission to speak and wait for it to be granted."

She had laughed nervously. "You're kidding, right?"

He glanced from the road to her face. "No. Dead serious." He warmed to his topic. "You'll be kept naked at all times, except when I dress you up for my amusement. You'll submit to my punishments without protest."

"Sam, this is nuts. I'm not into all this perverted S&M shit—"

"Nobody asked you what you're *into*, babe. This isn't designed for your pleasure. Don't forget, you bilked me out of a whole lot of money. You committed a crime—a felony that could land your ass in jail for a very long time. I'm willing to settle for thirty days, but those days will be on my terms. Not yours. My word, once we cross the threshold of my house, will become your law. You will exist solely to serve and please me. You will give up all free will. You will be my possession to use as I see fit."

He turned again to look at her. She was staring at him with her mouth open, her hands clenched tightly in her lap. "If you fuck up, Rae—if you don't behave—I'll cancel the deal and call the cops then and there. I want complete obedience and submission for the full thirty days. Are we one-hundred-percent crystal clear on this?"

Her miserable little nod had made him feel almost guilty—until he remembered the one-hundred-thirty-three thousand dollars she'd stolen.

Now as he saw her hesitation in opening her blouse, he said, "Don't make me repeat myself. I tell you to do something—you do it. Got it?"

He watched as she lifted her hands to the pearl buttons of her blouse. Her fingers were shaking as she opened them and she hesitated after the first three, casting him a pleading look. "Hurry up," he said. "It's nothing I haven't seen before." She flushed but kept at it, until she got all the buttons open. "Take off the blouse." She obeyed and he took it from her. "Now the skirt and your pantyhose." Sam could feel his cock swelling.

Rae wrapped her arms protectively over her breasts. "Arms at your sides," he said, watching the blush rising over her cheeks as she obeyed. "I haven't even made you take off that bra—yet."

A sense of the surreal settled over Sam. He had her! It had been nearly a year since he'd tasted those perfect lips, since he'd had that warm, yielding body beneath his. Now he had Rae Johansen as his personal sex slave for a month! Was he about to wake up from yet another dream? Or was this really happening?

He stuffed her clothes into the overnight bag he'd allowed her to pack. "Don't move. I'm going to get something and I'll be right back."

"Sam," she began, "this is crazy. Please, I—"

"You just earned yourself your first punishment. You know the rules. Now shut that pretty little mouth of yours and do as you're told."

Taking her purse and overnight bag with him, he left her standing there. He hadn't locked the front door and he was aware she could just turn tail and run, though how far she'd get without her purse or clothing was anyone's guess. Still, if she bailed he'd just blow the whistle and let the police deal with her like the common criminal she was.

He headed down into the basement he'd converted into a rather handy dungeon, filled with his favorite toys. Rummaging in the cupboard that contained his bondage gear, he found what he was looking for and returned to find Rae standing where he'd left her.

"This is your slave collar. It's a sign of ownership and, for this month, I own you. You will only remove it when I give permission." He showed Rae the black leather collar, a large metal ring hanging from the front of it. "Lift your hair so I can buckle it in place."

Rae's eyes widened but she did as she was told, gathering and lifting her hair. Sam buckled the collar around her long, slender neck and attached the dog leash he'd brought with him to the ring at her throat.

"What the hell—" she sputtered.

"Punishment number two," he interjected, which silenced her.

He jerked gently at the leash. "Time to show you to your home for the next thirty days." He led her down the basement stairs and watched her take in the room, her hand coming up to her mouth as she looked around at the equipment.

The basement was one large finished room with wall-to-wall carpeting and its own bathroom. There was even a bed in the corner of the large space, for when he wanted to make love to his chosen partner of the evening and they were too spent to make it up to the bedroom.

Rae's eyes were wide as she took in the St. Andrew's Cross, the wide padded sawhorse, the punishment chair, the stocks, the large, sturdy eyehooks bolted into the ceiling and the impressive array of whips, crops, paddles, floggers and rope hung at intervals on the walls.

Sam flashed to the one time he'd had her in his bed. She'd come hard while bound beneath him, gasping and sweating, her nipples like marbles as he squeezed and bit them. She'd rejected out of hand his suggestion of a gentle flogging, protesting a little too much that she wasn't into "whips and chains" and demanding to know what kind of girl he thought she was.

He was pretty sure he knew, but he hadn't pressed. She hadn't been ready, not then. He'd hoped to introduce her slowly to the fiery pleasures of BDSM play, but she'd ended things before they began. Now he had the chance of a lifetime. She was his, all his, for thirty glorious days.

He watched her gazing with wide-eyed fascination at his toys and couldn't help grinning with anticipation, though he felt almost sorry for her. But she'd agreed to the terms—thirty days in exchange for his not pressing charges for a very serious felony. She was getting off easy.

But not too easy — he'd see to that.

"I put your things in the bathroom," he said, "except your cell phone. I'll keep that safe for you." He patted his pocket. "I'll check your messages for you and run interference as necessary until you get back from Japan."

He smiled. She didn't smile back.

He'd stood over her shoulder while she sat at her laptop at her apartment, typing the email he dictated letting her family and friends know she was going on a trip to Japan for business, and would be back in four weeks. He'd allowed her to pack a few outfits and underwear, not that she would need any of it. He let her pack her makeup and the various things women couldn't seem to live without. Most important was her packet of birth control pills, since he planned on fucking her regularly, once she'd earned the privilege of his cock.

Sam rubbed his hands together. A part of him could scarcely believe she'd agreed to this setup. That same part could hardly believe he'd even come up with it. Was he really going to go through with it?

It had been a long-held and deep-seated fantasy of his to keep a woman captive in his dungeon, having his complete way with her. He had read a novel once about a guy who was obsessed with a movie star. The guy made all these elaborate plans to kidnap and keep her in his home in the country. He kept her there for months, locking her into a cage when he wasn't fucking or torturing her. The book had ignited something in Sam — a dark, dangerous part of his psyche that normally he kept well under wraps.

How far would he go with Rae?
How far did he dare?

~*~

"Take off the bra and panties. Now." Sam's voice was firm, the smile no longer on his face. Rae bit her lip. She felt frozen in place. He took a step toward her, his expression menacing. Instinctively she took a step back, but she reached behind herself to unhook her bra.

You can handle this, she told herself. *It's better than jail, way better.* She'd understood he was going to expect sex — that's what being a sex slave meant, wasn't it? At least she found him attractive and, if she were honest, the one time they'd been together had been explosive. Though she'd been put off by his kink, she couldn't deny the way her body had responded to what he was doing, even while her mind told her it was wrong.

She wasn't shy about her body. She told herself just to think of this as a date. A very long, very strange date in a room full of whips and chains. A shiver ran its way up her spine. She let her bra fall to the floor and stepped out of her panties. She started to cross her arms over her body but was stopped by his command.

"Arms at your sides. Never cover up in front of me, is that understood?"

She dropped her arms. "That was a direct question, Rae. You failed to answer. That's punishment number three. For a bright girl, you aren't too swift."

Rae had to bite on her tongue to keep from retorting that for a smart guy, he was a fucking prick. She was pretty sure *that* would earn her punishment number four. The bastard was smirking at her, clearly loving her discomfort and his control over her.

"You're slumping. Stand proud for me. Put your shoulders back," he ordered. She glanced at him, her lips pressed into a nervous line but he stared her down.
After a moment, she obeyed, lifting her shoulders, which caused her breasts to thrust forward.

Sam was looking her up and down, his eyes sweeping in a slow, insolent wave. He walked around her and stood close behind her, cupping one of her ass cheeks. She stiffened but didn't dare pull away. He moved closer, so his chest was against her back, and reached around her, cupping one of her breasts. He pulled gently at the nipple, which, in spite of the situation, stiffened at his touch.

She felt his breath warm against her neck as he leaned down, whispering, "Are you ready for punishment number one, Rae?"

Ready? Was it a trick question? Wait, it was a *direct* question, so she'd better answer quickly before she got another freaking demerit. "Um, I guess I don't really have a choice."

"That's correct. You don't." He stepped away and moved around her, walking toward the bed. "Your first punishment will be a good, old-fashioned spanking." He sat and patted the bed. "Come on over here and lie across my lap."

Rae stared at him, her body rooted to the spot. She couldn't seem to move, even if she'd wanted to. Her heart was pounding and her breathing was shallow.

Sam regarded her, a half-smile playing over his lips. He shook his head. "Rae, Rae, Rae," he said with mock distress. "What am I going to do with you? You can't even follow the most basic command."

He had unclipped the dog leash from her collar when they'd entered the dungeon. Now he stood and strode toward her and she saw he still had it in his hand. Before she could react, he clipped it to the collar and yanked, sending her stumbling forward. He walked briskly toward the bed, jerking her along like a naughty puppy as she cried out with dismay.

He sat again and pulled her unceremoniously across his lap while she squirmed and struggled, too frightened to be still. With sheer brute force he held her down, a hand on the back of her neck, his other arm wrapped over her thighs, pinning her in place.

"Calm down." His voice was almost soothing though his grip remained tight. "I'm not going to let you go until you calm down and stay still. You earned this spanking and then some." The hand on the back of her neck tightened and his voice was a warning. "I'm starting to think you weren't sincere. Should we just end this now and I'll give the NYPD a call?"

"No!" Rae cried breathlessly. "No, I'll be good. I promise. I'm just—I'm scared. You're really freaking me out, Sam." The enormity of what she'd signed up for hit her all at once and, though she knew it wasn't going to do any good in the end, Rae couldn't seem to stop herself. She started to struggle again, determined to wriggle off his lap and then make a run for it.

"Damn it, Rae!" Sam lifted her and tossed her onto the bed. He wrestled her down, grabbing her wrists and yanking her arms over her head. He crouched beside her on the bed, pressing her wrists hard into the mattress. "Let's put an end to this bullshit here and now. You will stick to the terms of our agreement or I'll call the whole thing off, got it? I'm warning you, this is your last chance to behave. Then it's back to embezzlement charges and an orange jumpsuit for you."

He loosened his grip on her wrists, but kept his large hands wrapped around them. "What's it going to be, Rae? Your choice."

There was no choice and he knew it. That's how blackmail worked, she wanted to shout at him. She managed to hold her tongue, however, and nodded meekly. "I'll behave," she said in a tiny voice.

He glowered at her a moment longer, but at last his expression eased. He let go of her wrists and unclipped the leash from the collar around her neck. Instinctively she reached for the collar, touching the stiff leather as he maneuvered himself again to sit on the edge of the bed.

He twisted back to look at her. "All right then. We'll try this again. You're going to get the spanking you deserve. Not a playful sexy swatting, but a bona fide spanking reserved for naughty little brats. I've half a mind to use a belt, but since this is your first punishment, we'll start easy."

Rae swallowed, desperately trying to think of a way out of this, but she gave up as the frown began to return to Sam's face. She scooted along the bed, draping herself awkwardly over his lap, her heart smacking at her sternum. She pressed her face into the bed, her entire body tense with dreaded anticipation.

She felt his hand on her ass and jerked, but instead of spanking her, he began to stroke the skin, moving his hands lightly over her ass, thighs and lower back. She remained tensed, her muscles taut, her hands clenched into fists, but he only continued to stroke and soothe her. After a while, despite her fear, she found herself relaxing, at least a little. Her fingers unfurled and she let out the breath she hadn't realized she'd been holding.

"That's it." Sam's voice was soothing though his words were not. "Take what's coming. This is nothing compared to what I'm going to expect of you soon."

Rae tensed again. Were those words supposed to offer her comfort? Maybe they weren't. Maybe he'd been deliberate in relaxing her with his touch, in lulling her into a false sense of ease just so he could turn up the tension again.

All at once the soothing touch was replaced by a sharp sting as his hand came down hard across her left ass cheek. Rae yelped and jerked on his lap, instinctively bringing her hands back to cover the patch of fire he'd left on her skin. Sam smacked at her hands until she pulled them away.

"Don't do that again," he warned, "or I'll tie you down. Never block me when you're being punished. Do you understand?"

Rae didn't answer. Three sharp blows, even harder than the first, followed in quick succession. "Answer the question."

"Yes! Yes, I—I understand," Rae managed to gasp. She gripped the bedspread, clutching the fabric in both hands to keep from covering her ass as Sam's hard palm left streaks of pain over every inch of her bottom.

"Please, please, you have to stop! It hurts! You're hurting me!"

"That's the point. You're being punished. It's supposed to hurt. And you spoke without asking for permission." He smacked the backs of her thighs, one after the other as she cried out with pain, wriggling on his lap in a vain effort to twist her body away from the stinging blows.

She began whimpering between yelps, her skin on fire, her body slick with sweat from the struggle and the fear. He was relentless, smacking her ass and thighs until finally she gave up, too stunned and exhausted to squirm.

As she lay still over his lap she became aware of the hard press of his erection beneath her. He got hard from hitting her, the sick fuck! While she mulled this over in her outraged mind, something strange was happening in her body. The pain of a moment before seemed almost to ebb away. She could still feel the blows, but the sting was gone. Probably a neurologic reaction of her nerve endings to protect her by making her go numb, she supposed. Whatever the reason, this freed her to focus more on the hard cock that was thrust urgently against her with each smack of his palm.

She remembered that cock — large and thick and hard as smooth, satin-covered steel when it had entered her. In spite of the bizarre situation in which she found herself, she felt her pussy moistening, a tug from deep inside causing her to shift a bit on his lap. He shifted in turn against her, his thigh pressing up between her legs, forcing them to spread.

He stopped smacking her, now running his hands in slow circles over the heated flesh of her ass and thighs. "Let's take your temperature," he said, his voice low and throaty, his cock twitching beneath her.

She didn't understand what he meant, until he slid a finger down along the crack of her ass, stopping at her pussy. He probed lightly and pressed harder, the tip of his finger slipping inside her. She tried to close her legs but he stopped her with his knee.

"Don't you *dare* close your legs. Your body is mine to use, did you forget already?" He pushed the finger in deeper. "Hot little cunt. You're wet, you slut. So much for all your pretend outrage and disgust—you got off on having your ass spanked." There was triumph in his voice.

Rae felt her face heat almost as hot as her ass. "I did *not!*" she shouted, before remembering his stupid fucking rule about not speaking unless asked a direct question. She bit her lip at her transgression but he seemed to let it pass.

Again she tried to close her legs and this time he smacked her pussy, making her yelp with pain and surprise. "What did I tell you? Spread your legs as wide as you can, slut. That's my cunt, not yours. Get that straight quick or I'll give you a whipping with a single tail that'll make the spanking seem like a tickle in comparison."

Frightened by both the threat and the tone in his voice, Rae went limp against him, allowing her thighs to fall open. Her heart was racing and she couldn't stop the tremor that moved through her when his finger again sought and found her entrance, pushing its way inside her.

After a moment he withdrew his finger and rubbed lightly over her clit, moving in easy circles that she had to admit felt good. Again he laughed that soft, superior laugh that made her want to slug him. He added a finger, pushing both deep into her until she groaned, unable to stop the clamping of her muscles against the invading digits.

"Yeah," he said, his voice husky. "That's it, babe. Work it. Show me what a little whore you really are." He did something with his hand so he was both inside her and rubbing her clit. She moaned, unable to stop her hips moving in a grind against his hand.

What was he *doing* to her? She groaned again, grabbing handfuls of the bedspread and hiding her face in the folds. Each time he swiveled his fingers inside her he was touching *something*—it was almost like she had a second clit inside, only it was different—the sensation more intense, deeper somehow, each time he strummed that sweet spot.

Was this the G-spot she'd heard of but never really believed existed? Certainly no other man had ever found it, that was for damn sure. Jesus god, it felt so fucking good! She groaned again, and again he chuckled. Fuck him, why shouldn't she take the pleasure when it was offered? She'd endured enough to get it! She gave herself over to the sensations, letting them fill her mind and body with a sweet, white heat that left her burning for his touch.

He was as relentless with his fingers inside her as he'd been with his hand on her ass. Over the roar of blood in her ears, dimly she heard Sam bark, "Don't come. You may not come."

Was he joking? She must have heard it wrong. And anyway, if he didn't want her to come, he'd better stop whatever the hell it was he was doing to her. Oh, god, it felt good. So incredibly, amazingly intense, like nothing she'd ever experienced. She no longer even tried to control the writhing and shuddering of her body as he wrested the powerful reaction from deep within her.

"Fuck. Oh, god, yes, *fuck*!" she heard herself shouting as her body went suddenly rigid, impaled against his hand. Beyond control, she began to thrust and gyrate as spirals of fierce, nearly intolerable pleasure wracked through her body.

When she was finally able to stop the trembling that had overtaken her, she lay like a rag doll, her legs akimbo, her head hanging half off the bed. His fingers were still buried inside her. He moved them just slightly, but it was enough to set off a series of tiny convulsive shudders, aftershocks of the intense orgasm. Maybe, it slowly occurred to her, it wouldn't be quite so terrible to be this man's "sex slave" for the next thirty days.

He pulled his hand away, but she felt too limp, too sated, to move. Standing, he leaned over her, slipping his arms beneath her and lifting her from the bed. He set her down none too gently on the floor.

"Kneel," he commanded. "Get on your knees, forehead touching the carpet. Go on, move!"

His words penetrated the endorphin-induced fog, the words burning it away. Though her limbs were heavy from the powerful orgasm, she didn't dare disobey. As she scrambled into the humiliating position, he said, "I told you not to come. It was a direct order."

Rae lifted her head. "I couldn't help it. Whatever you were doing, it was just—I couldn't stop my body. If you didn't want me to come you shouldn't have—"

Sam knelt suddenly beside her, jerking her head back sharply by the hair. She cried out but he kept his fingers entwined in her hair. "Don't you tell me what I should or shouldn't do," he hissed. "You will learn to control your body. You will come when I tell you and not a moment sooner, no matter what is happening to you. You are my property now. My sex slave. You do my bidding. I decide, not you. Do you understand?"

It was a direct question.

"Yes," she managed. "I understand."

And to think, a moment before she'd thought this wouldn't be so bad.

Chapter 3

"Kneel up, hands behind your head, knees spread wide so I can see your cunt."

Sam stood over Rae, his cock throbbing at the sight of the naked girl at his feet. She was one of those women who was always perfectly put together, her hair hanging in a glossy curtain just to her shoulders, the flawless makeup, the shiny lips as forbidden as Eve's apple, the supple curves of her youthful body hidden in linen and silk tailored to taunt without revealing much.

Now she was his—naked and at his mercy, her hair tousled, mascara smudged beneath her eyes, no trace of lipstick on that pouty mouth. She stared up at him, biting her full lower lip, the fear in her eyes like an aphrodisiac.

When she didn't react immediately to his dictate, Sam bent down, again seizing a fist of hair to jerk her upright. Rae gasped, a small cry of pain that made his cock harden. He forced her into position, pulling her arms and jerking them up.

"Hands behind your head, fingers locked together." He moved to stand directly in front of her, using his foot to push her thighs apart, forcing her to expose her trimmed pussy. Her face was flushing a deep pink and her dark blue eyes flashed daggers. He would break down her defiant resistance soon enough.

"This position is called kneeling up, and when I give the order, you obey without hesitation." He crouched in front of her, leaning close so their faces were nearly touching. She leaned away and he slapped her cheek, not too hard, but hard enough to make her cry out. She dropped her hands, putting them up as if to ward off a blow.

He wasn't surprised at this completely undisciplined reaction; indeed, he had expected it. "Back into position," he ordered, his voice low, its power palpable.

"Sam, you're scaring—"

"The rules. No speaking unless—"

"I can't do this!" Rae hugged herself, rocking on her knees. She looked up at him with tears in her eyes, her mouth trembling. "Please, Sam. Can't we work something out? I want to please you, to—to serve you, but you're scaring me. Please..."

If she'd been his lover, he would have scooped her up into his arms and kissed her, whispering that she was his lovely, brave girl who could do this for him, for them. But she wasn't his lover. She was being punished, and had to learn to obey.

This was the moment to establish his complete dominance and make it quite clear just who was in charge. "You *will* please me," he informed her. "And you will serve me. On my terms, not yours. Despite your promise to obey, in just the short time you've been in my dungeon you've proved yourself worthless. You're untrained and disobedient at every turn. You're begging for punishment. You've made it abundantly clear that you can't or won't follow the simplest of commands."

He reached down, pulling her to her feet by one arm. Roughly he hauled her along toward the St. Andrew's cross. She cried out, struggling in earnest as he forced her against the wooden X frame, but she was no match for his strength. He positioned her facing outward, her lower back resting against the intersection of the crossed wood, which would give him ample access to her ass as well. It wasn't long before he had her properly restrained, her wrists bound high over her head, her legs stretched wide and secured at the ankles by thick leather straps.

He stepped back, watching her. Her chest was heaving, her tears leaving black trails of mascara along her cheeks, her hair falling into her face. He crossed his arms over his chest and let her cry.

He waited until her sobs subsided into hiccupping whimpers before approaching her. Gently he smoothed her hair back from her face, tucking it behind her ears. Using his thumb, he wiped the tears from her cheeks. She turned her head away at his touch, closing her eyes.

"Rae, look at me."

Slowly she turned her head toward him, but kept her eyes lowered. He put a hand on her throat, forefinger and thumb just below her jaw line, forcing her head up. His grip was light, only a slight pressure, but enough to make the point that, if he wanted to, he could choke the life out of her.

"Look at me," he commanded again. "Now."

Slowly she looked up, meeting his gaze. Her lashes were wet with tears. Sam kept his hand at her throat as he stared into her eyes, searching for the spark. There was fear, yes, and still the fire of defiance, but beneath it—something else?

He cupped her breasts, one in each hand. They were perfect, round and heavy, the heft pleasing in his hands. The nipples perked like the dark pink tips of number two pencils, perfect for clamping. One day soon, when she was further along in her training, he would have her offer her breasts to him. She would hold them up and beg for the cut of the cane against the soft, creamy skin.

For now he contented himself with tweaking her nipples, pulling them taut and savoring the swell as they engorged at his touch. Leaning down, he flicked her right nipple with his tongue, drawing a circle in the puckering skin around it before lightly biting the hard nubbin. He pulled it with his teeth, just hard enough to elicit a small, delicious gasp of pain. He did the same to her other nipple, leaving them both erect.

Using his middle finger, he stroked along her cleft, lightly teasing her clit, then pushing inside her. He felt the involuntary clamp of her vaginal muscles around his finger. Gently he moved inside her, feeling the walls moisten and heat.

On an impulse he leaned down again, kissing her mouth. She kept her lips closed until he pried them apart, forcing his way between them with his tongue. She submitted—what choice did she have—but she didn't kiss him back.

No matter. She wasn't his lover.

She was his slave.

His possession. His to use, to train, to discipline and to punish.

"It's time, Rae. It's time for punishment number two."

~*~

Sam stepped back, his eyes on her as his fingers moved down his shirt, opening the buttons. He pulled it off, revealing his broad muscular chest. He unbuckled his belt, pulling it through the loops. He folded the belt in half and flicked it in the air, creating a snapping sound that made Rae jump.

As he moved closer, Rae gasped and turned her head away, screwing her eyes tight, her hands curled into fists of fear over her head. She expected to feel the sharp sting of the leather belt against her body, but instead she felt it being pressed against her throat, just above the collar already in place. She opened her eyes in surprise, only to realize he was binding it around her neck, buckling it behind her around the wood, restraining her by the throat. The belt was thicker than the collar beneath it, the leather tight and constricting.

Rae realized she was panting, her breath coming in rapid, shallow gasps. "Please," she begged. "Let me down. I can't do this. Please…"

Sam didn't reply. He left her, walking across the space toward a large cabinet. Rae strained to see what he was doing, barely able to turn her head within the confines of the belt at her throat.

He returned with what looked like a small whip. He flicked it in the air near her and Rae startled, jerking in her restraints. She coughed as the belt, tight at her throat, pressed against her larynx from her sudden movement.

"Why are you being punished, Rae?"

"Please, let me down—"

The movement was sudden. He struck her cheek with his open hand, the sound sharp and explosive in her ear. "Another fucking word that isn't a direct response to a question and I'll gag you, got it? You aren't going to be let down until you're done receiving your punishment. Now answer the question. Why are you being punished?"

"I—I don't know." Rae's mind was whirling, her heart beating high in her throat.

Sam leaned in close so she could feel his breath on her cheek. She tried to turn her head away, but the belt restricted the movement. She closed her eyes.

"It's because you spoke out of turn, Rae. You can't seem to keep your fucking mouth shut."

He stepped back, again flicking the whip in the air, the leather braid so close she could feel the swish of air it caused near her thigh. In spite of her fear, Rae stared at the little whip, mesmerized. At last she tore her gaze away to look at Sam, who was smiling, a slow, easy smile that would have been sexy if his eyes weren't so hard.

"You said this morning I couldn't just tie you up and give you thirty lashes, remember?"

Was it really only this morning? Only this morning that she'd awoken, thinking about how in just another few weeks she'd finally be out of the jam she'd backed herself into? Was it only this morning she'd blithely sailed into Sam's office, only to be blindsided by his accusations and ultimatums?

Another slap to her cheek jerked Rae back to the present. "Answer. The. Question."

"Yes!" Rae gasped. "Yes, I remember."

"And you were wrong, weren't you?"

God, I fucking hate you. "Yes."

Sam nodded, cocking an eyebrow. "Thirty days, thirty lashes. I like it. That's what you'll get now. Thirty lashes, one for each day you are here. You'll count for me. Count out loud each stroke of the whip you so richly deserve."

He flicked the tail so suddenly she didn't even realize he'd done it until the line of fire moved over her thigh. "Ow!" she cried.

~ 47 ~

"Count!" he barked.

"One! Ow! Two!" The second stroke licked her other thigh, leaving a trail of pain.

He moved behind her, the crack of the leather against her ass making her jump in the split second before the pain registered in her brain. "Fuck!" she screamed.

"Fuck is not a number," Sam replied, his tone amused. "So we start again at one."

Rage edged its way past fear at that moment. If she could have, she would have strangled him. Instead, as the whip curled cruelly around her left thigh, she cried, "One!"

Ten more blows, five on each ass cheek, though the order was random. Each time the leather struck, Rae jerked against her restraints and cried out, the belt at her throat choking her. Desperately she tried to keep count, calling out the numbers, tears of impotent fury coursing down her cheeks.

He returned to face her. This time the lash caught the underside of one of her breasts, snaking over the skin. Rae screamed.

"Count," Sam hissed.

"Twelve," Rae cried quickly, terrified he'd make her start over. "Please," she entreated. The whip struck, finding her other breast. She screamed, unable to help it, but she managed to gasp, "Thirteen."

He struck her thighs, a stripe of fire on each leg before again moving behind her. For a while he concentrated on her ass, which was easier to tolerate than anywhere else, though it still stung plenty. At twenty-eight he returned to stand in front of her. She was breathing hard, dizzy with pain and fear, her body slicked with sweat.

"The last two," Sam said. "And then you'll thank me for taking the time to correct you."

The flick was sudden, the pain excruciating as the tip of the whip made contact with Rae's right nipple. She howled, forgetting to count, forgetting language altogether. Then her left nipple exploded with pain.

Her heart was thundering in her ears, her breath coming in ragged gasps. "Count," she heard him admonish, as if from a distance, though his mouth was close to her ear.

Somehow she forced her lips to comply, desperate for this to be over. "Twenty-nine," she whispered. "Thirty."

When he unbuckled the belt, her head fell forward, her hair hanging down in her face. He crouched down and released the ankle cuffs. Her knees sagged, the weight of her body pulling hard against her wrists.

She slumped against Sam when her wrists were freed, her arms flopping down. Sam pulled her forward but then let her go, forcing her to her knees. He stood in front of her as she swayed on her haunches, trying to clear the whirling fog in her brain.

"Now you'll thank me for the punishment you so richly deserved," Sam intoned above her. His crotch was level with her face and she couldn't help but the see the erection tenting his pants. She watched as he slid the zipper down and drew both the pants and his underwear along his muscular thighs.

His cock was as she remembered, thick and long above heavy balls. She could smell his musk, which mingled with the sharp scent of her own sweat and fear. She understood what he wanted her to do, of course she did.

She wanted to smack the offending shaft, or better, to grab hold of his testicles and twist until he screamed. Of course she didn't dare. Not while she was here, his voluntary prisoner. Why the hell had she agreed to his insane conditions?

It's only thirty days, she reminded herself. One short month and then he'd set her free. They'd sign the indemnifying agreement and she could move on with her life, or what was left of it.

"Kneel up," he ordered, his cock bobbing inches from her face.

Rae turned the words over in her mind, trying to remember what kneeling up meant. Hands behind her head, yes, that was it. She lifted her hands and as she locked her fingers behind her neck she looked down, drawing in her breath sharply as she saw the angry red welts across her breasts and the tops of her thighs.

"Spread your knees wider." Sam moved closer, his legs between hers forcing them farther apart. "No hands. Keep them behind your head. Now thank me properly, cunt. Do it like you mean it. If you do a good job, I'll let you rest."

Rae glanced toward the bed in the corner of the room. Her muscles were rigid and exhausted from the stress of all she'd endured to this moment. The bedding looked soft and inviting, the pillows plump. Oh, to rest—her body ached with fatigue. To sleep—a brief escape from the nightmare in which she found herself.

Sam nudged the head of his cock against her lips. Rae's impulse was to keep her lips firmly closed. Did he really expect her to suck him off as a *thank you* for whipping her? And yet, what choice did she have? What would he do to her if she refused? She was helpless, completely and utterly at his mercy. At least, once she'd satisfied the bastard, he'd let her rest.

She parted her lips, allowing him to thrust his cock between them. It lay heavy and warm in her mouth, the head nudging back toward her throat. She began to suckle and lick, closing her eyes, trying to pretend he was her lover, rather than her jailer.

If only she could use her hands, she'd be able to get him off much quicker. Still, she was skilled at pleasing a man. She'd make him come as fast as she could. She'd capitalize on his being a guy—once he came, he'd finally leave her the fuck alone.

She focused on her task, grimly pleased when she heard him softly groan above her. She licked along the shaft, creating suction with her lips and tongue as best she could. He groaned again, thrusting forward as his hands dropped heavily to her shoulders, holding her in place.

He eased his cock in and out of her mouth and she did her best to use her lips and tongue to increase the friction and the pleasure as he moved. "Yeah," he breathed, his voice throaty and deep. She struggled to stay in position as his movements quickened. He was breathing fast, thrusting in and out of her mouth and she knew it was just a matter of seconds now, please god, until he came.

He shuddered and she tensed, readying herself for the spurt of his ejaculate. Hopefully he'd shoot it right down her throat and all she'd have to do was swallow without having to taste it.

All at once he let go of her shoulders, pulling his cock out of her mouth. Her eyes, which had been closed, flew open with surprise. He was gripping the shiny shaft in his fist, pulling at his cock, his eyes fixed on her face. He groaned once more and, before she realized what was happening, shot his load in white ribbons over her cheeks and lips, the last few globs landing on her breasts.

Surprise and humiliation burned their way through Rae in equal measure. Instinctively she brought her hand forward to wipe the sticky mess from her lips.

"Back in position!" Sam barked. "How dare you move before being given permission?"

Hating him with every fiber of her being, but too afraid to find out what would happen if she disobeyed, Rae reluctantly left the mess on her face and breasts and put her hands back behind her head. She looked down at the carpet as Sam tucked his cock back into his trousers and zipped them up.

She didn't move as he stepped away from her. She heard the grating sound of metal on metal and stole a glance toward the corner of the room where Sam stood. He was bending over a large black metal crate, a cage to keep a large animal or, she realized with dawning dread, a person.

Sam turned to look at her. "Crawl over here."

Rae stared at him. Crawl? Had she heard him correctly? As if reading her mind, he reiterated, "That's right. On your hands and knees. Move it."

Rae lowered her arms, again reaching to wipe the come splashed on her face. "Leave it," Sam said. "Let it dry there. A reminder that you're my property. Now, crawl over here right now unless you'd rather have punishment number three first."

Dismayed and frightened, Rae dropped to all fours and began to crawl toward her captor, her bare breasts swaying as she made the humiliating trek toward him. He pulled the door of the cage open and pointed inside.

"Get in there. You haven't earned the bed yet."

In spite of herself, Rae shrank back. She opened her mouth to protest, but shut it again, the stinging memory of the lash looming large in her mind and on her skin.

Sam pointed emphatically toward the cage. Reluctantly, Rae crawled into the small space, shrinking back as he closed and padlocked the gate behind her. The bottom of the cage was padded with about an inch of foam rubber bound in plastic sheeting and covered in a thin layer of cotton fabric.

"Rest while you can," Sam said. "I'll be back later to check on you."

"Wait!" Rae cried breathlessly. "I mean, um, please, can I have permission to speak?"

Sam regarded her for a long moment, an amused expression on his face. Finally he nodded slowly. "You may."

Rae drew in a breath. How could she get herself out of this horrid little cage? "Please," she begged. "You can't leave me here in this thing! I have to pee. And I'm thirsty. And I don't like small spaces. Please, don't leave me here alone!"

Sam shook his head, his tone filled with mock sympathy. "Poor thing. I guess you should have thought of all this before you stole from me. As to your creature comforts, you should be more observant. You've got everything you need right there."

He pointed toward the back of the cage where two bottles hung, one in each corner. The first was an empty plastic bottle with a wide neck opening into a square container. It was, she realized, a female urinal. She was expected to pee in *that*?

In the other corner there hung an upside down water bottle with a tiny metal spout, the kind of thing used in hamster cages, only quite a bit larger. She was expected to suck on the tip like a rodent in a cage. She was, she knew, thirsty enough to do it, but not while he was watching, the prick.

"I've got the monitor on and I'll be listening. I don't want to hear a sound, unless it's an emergency, got it?" Without waiting for a response, Sam turned away. She could hear his tread on the basement stairs and then she was alone.

Rae waited, still and silent as a mouse for several long moments, until the pressure in her bladder spurred her to action. She reached for the urinal and popped off the cap. Awkwardly she positioned herself over it, willing her tense muscles to relax enough to allow her to pee. Finally the pee rushed forth in a hot stream, splashing slightly as she adjusted the lip of the urinal to catch it.

She capped the bottle and hung it again on the side of the cage, looking around for something to wipe herself with. Finding nothing, she used the edge of the sheet that covered the padding. She scooted away toward the other bottle. At first she tried to get it off the cage so she could hold it in her hands, but it was securely bolted in place with tiny padlocks. The bastard had thought of everything.

It took a while to position herself so her mouth was at the proper angle to suck the spigot, but finally she managed. The water felt good going down, soothing her parched throat. Once she'd had enough to slake the worst of her thirst, she realized she was starving. Sam had gotten them both burgers at a drive thru on the way from her place to his, but she hadn't been able to get down a single bite.

She pushed against her empty stomach, looking down at her naked body. The welts were still there, long, angry lines of red where he'd whipped her. His come had dried on her breasts and face. Disgusted, she pushed at the tip of the water bottle with her finger, using a little to rub at the ejaculate. *Better not waste the water*, she warned herself, and gave up her efforts.

The cage was nearly tall enough to sit up in, but it was easier to curl into a ball. She hugged herself, tears leaking from the corners of her eyes. She was tired, so, so tired. Not that she could sleep, locked up in this crate like an animal! But at least she could rest, close her tired eyes and let her aching muscles recover as much as possible before the bastard returned with more torture and humiliation.

She closed her eyes.

And somehow, she slept.

Chapter 4

The sound insinuated itself into troubled dreams, pulling her toward consciousness. The sound of a thunder clap, a gun's report, a snapping whip...

Rae's eyes flew open. It was the sound of a whip, though the crack was much sharper and louder than the small single tail he'd used on her earlier. Her heart began at once to flutter and constrict in her chest. Her left arm was trapped and numb beneath her body, which was curled into a fetal position on the floor of the animal cage where he'd left her.

The whip continued to snap somewhere out of her range of vision, making her wince. She struggled into a sort of sitting crouch, her neck bent to keep from hitting the top of the cage with her head. The cracking sound suddenly ceased.

He had heard her.

She froze, not even daring to breathe. After a few moments she peered through the bars of the cage. She could see nothing from her corner except the door that led to the basement stairs. She heard the tread of his footsteps and a moment later his booted feet appeared. Her eyes followed the line of his long legs, now covered in soft black leather that molded to his muscular calves and thighs and the bulge at his crotch. She drew in her breath, aroused in spite of herself.

She could see his face through the bars that made up the ceiling of her cage. His blond hair looked damp and freshly combed. Rae longed for a shower herself. Her skin was itchy with dried sweat and his sticky come, her hair tangled around her face. She needed to pee again and her mouth tasted sour.

"Have a nice nap?" His tone was light, as if he had entered the bedroom of a friend who was just waking.

An angry retort rose to her lips but she managed to bite it back just in time. *Direct question*, a small voice whispered and so she hurriedly said, "I guess I fell asleep," hoping that counted as an answer.

"Hungry?"

The question was like a key that unlocked her completely empty stomach. "Starving," she admitted. How long had she been there? How long had she slept?

He crouched in front of the cage. "I've made some dinner. I had mine already but I saved you some. Steak, salad, some fresh corn. I have a nice bottle of Cabernet opened. Sound good?"

Rae's mouth pooled with saliva at the mention of the food. "Yes. Yes, please," she said eagerly, reaching to grip the bars of the cage. Surely he'd let her out now? Let her eat?

He reached for the padlock and unlocked it. Releasing the latch, he let the gate swing outward. Standing again, he stepped back.

Rae crawled out of the cramped space, keenly aware of her nudity and disheveled appearance, and the fact she was on her knees. She started to rise but his hand on her shoulder held her down.

"You don't get up until I tell you."

She stiffened but stayed down, the thought of steak and red wine keeping her still.

Sam spoke over her head as she focused on his black square-toed boots. "Before you earn the privilege of a meal, there is the little matter of punishment number three."

Rae's heart sank at this unwelcome pronouncement. Still she kept her head down, too hungry to protest.

Sam's hand extended into her line of vision, held out as if for her to take it. Tentatively she reached for it and he pulled her upright. She swayed, dizziness nearly overcoming her. Sam's grip was tight and he brought an arm around her shoulders, steadying her.

"Do you need to use the bathroom?" He kept his arm still around her. Despite herself, she leaned into him. The silk of his black shirt was soft against her skin. She could smell a hint of his woodsy cologne.

"Yes," she replied, silently praying he didn't make her use the cage urinal in front of him. To her relief he guided her to the small bathroom and let her relieve herself in relative privacy, though he didn't allow her to close the door. As she washed her hands and splashed water over her face, she noted there was no mirror in the bathroom.

Sam stuck his head in the door, startling her. "Come out. You've had enough time." Having no choice, she obeyed him. Sam led her to the center of the dungeon. "Stand at attention, feet shoulder-width apart," he ordered. "Hands behind your head, same as for the kneeling up."

Feeling ridiculous, naked as she was, Rae had no choice but to comply. She felt the collar when she laced her fingers behind her neck, the metal buckle poking against her palms.

He stepped back. She stayed still, eyes focused on the carpet. "While I was showering and cooking dinner," Sam said, "I got to thinking about what would help you get accustomed more quickly to your situation."

He lifted his hand to her face and Rae stiffened, afraid he was going to slap her, but he only reached for a tendril of her hair, which he tucked behind one ear. He ran the back of one finger along her cheek — a gesture that would have been erotic or tender in other circumstances — but which now only frightened her.

He lowered his finger, drawing it down her throat and over the swell of her right breast, tracing a slow, lingering circle around the nipple at its center. "I'm going to help you get into a more submissive mindset so you don't keep banging your head against the wall of your disobedience and willfulness."

Reaching into his back pocket, Sam took out the dog leash. He clipped it to Rae's collar and tugged gently. "Keep your hands in position and follow me." He led her to a corner of the room to stand beside the short padded sawhorse. The spine, wider than Rae was used to seeing, was covered in soft black leather, the adjustable legs made of sturdy metal.

"Bend over onto the bondage horse. I built it myself, extra wide and sturdy for your comfort while I whip you." He chuckled at his own remark while Rae's blood ran cold with fear. She noted it was only about half the length of a typical sawhorse, just right for accommodating the upper half of a person's body as they bent forward.

What was he going to do to her? Instinctively she shrank back, dropping her hands from behind her head and wrapping them protectively around herself. "Please, Sam—"

Sam fixed Rae with his penetrating gaze. "Do as you're told," he said quietly. His voice was calm but there was no mistaking the steel beneath it. He jerked lightly at her leash, pulling her forward. "You disobey one more time, you speak out of turn again, and no food or drink tonight. Just back in the cage."

Rae swallowed hard, her mouth dry, her heart beating like a drum. She moved hesitantly, bending over the sawhorse as he'd instructed. She felt Sam's hand on her back, forcing her down onto the padded bench that pressed against her stomach and nestled between her breasts.

"Spread your legs so they line up with the back legs of the sawhorse. Grip the front legs to keep your balance." Rae wrapped her fingers around the cold metal, horribly aware of her splayed sex and asshole, exposed by the position into which he'd forced her. There was just room to rest her cheek against the soft, cool leather at the end of the padded bench.

She could hear Sam behind her and a moment later he was kneeling beside her, rope in his hand. He wrapped the rope around her left ankle, binding her to the sawhorse leg. He moved to the other leg and then to each wrist, wrapping the thin rope around and around until Rae was thoroughly tethered to the sawhorse and completely immobile. She felt the tremble of her body and the beating of her heart. Her breath was ragged in her throat and when she felt his hand glide along her back, Rae couldn't stop the yelp of fear that leaped from her mouth.

"Sensory deprivation," Sam said, waiting a beat, as if this was supposed to mean something to Rae. He continued. "The elimination of certain sensory perceptions can heighten a specific experience. You can't move or resist me in any way. Now we'll take away the senses, one by one."

He stepped closer and reached down. "Lift your head a little and open your mouth." As Rae tried to comply, Sam pressed his fingers past her lips, forcing her jaws apart. Before she realized what he was doing, he'd shoved a rubber ball into her mouth, which forced her tongue back, completely gagging her.

A wave of panic surged through her and she jerked hard in her ropes, but was unable to move, bound securely as she was. She could feel him buckling the ball gag behind her head and she tried to catch his eye, to beg him with her pleading expression not to do this, but all she could see was his crotch and muscular thighs beneath the black leather.

She saw him reach into his shirt pocket. He pulled out two little orange cylinders. It took her a moment to figure out what they were, but she realized all too soon, as he pressed one into each of her ears.

Finally he placed a sleep mask over her eyes. She was deaf, mute and blind, completely tied down, her ass and cunt fully exposed. She could hear the blood whooshing through her ears, pulsing in time to her heartbeat. The enormity of her vulnerability fully registered and Rae began to shake convulsively against the sawhorse. She was gripping the metal legs so hard her hands felt melded to them, the fingers paralyzed into position.

She jerked as she felt Sam's hands moving over her back and ass, her heart kicking into high gear. But instead of hurting her, his touch was soothing. He stroked her skin, moving in slow circles along her back and ass. She could feel his fingers, strong and sure, kneading her flesh, coaxing the rigidly clenched muscles beneath the skin to ease.

He massaged her shoulders and moved in a line with his fingers along either side of her spine. He lingered at her lower back, working out the tension until, in spite of her predicament, Rae found herself relaxing and the hammer of fear in her chest slowed to a steady pulse.

She felt his hands moving lightly over her ass, stroking the flesh, traveling downward toward her thighs and then back up again. She couldn't see or hear him, or anticipate where he would touch her next. When his finger moved lightly over her bared asshole, instinctively she tried, but of course failed, to close her legs.

The finger continued down, swirling lightly over her spread sex, gently touching the exposed folds. The finger was withdrawn and then returned, its tip now wet as it stroked in a tightening circle toward her entrance.

Rae moaned against her gag as the finger pressed inside her. In spite of her fear, his touch was electric, tickling alive every nerve ending as he moved in and out of her, sliding up with a whisper soft touch to her clit, which she could feel swell in response.

The memory of their one time together, when he'd convinced her to let him tie her wrists to the posts of the headboard while he fucked her, filtered into her brain. She'd come so hard, so many times that she'd lost count as he'd licked, fingered and fucked her to orgasm again and again. While her mind had rejected the rope and his dominant persona, her body had bucked and arched, out of control as he wrested every ounce of pleasure from her.

When her cooler head had prevailed, she'd told him afterwards that she wasn't into his scene, that it was better they just remain friends. When he'd had the gall to tell her she *needed* what he offered, she'd laughed it off, assuring him it had been an interesting experiment, but not one she cared to repeat. He'd looked at her long and hard, as if he could see behind her words to what lay beneath, but she'd shaken off his gaze, flipping her hair and turning away.

He'd let her go.

Now Sam's fingers continued to move in and around Rae's sex until she began to shudder in her restraints, an orgasm mounting and twisting inside her as she mewled against the ball wedged between her teeth. The climax crested and broke as she pulled hard against the ropes that held her bound and splayed. She lay in the silence and the dark, her heart smashing against the leather and beating in her ears.

All at once she felt something cold and wet against her asshole. She felt Sam's finger moving in a circle around the rim and then entering her nether hole. She felt her face heat at the thought of him staring down at her spread ass cheeks, his finger invading the virgin space. She stiffened, unable to close her legs as something slick and hard pressed its way past the tight sphincter.

She felt the invading phallus push slowly but inexorably into her. It didn't hurt too much until the last bit, which felt like a fist pushing its way into her. Every muscle in her body was clenched with pain and fear. She squealed ineffectually against her gag and then sagged against the sawhorse, thoroughly humiliated and exhausted.

More lubricant was applied to her spread pussy, still highly sensitive from the recent strong orgasm. Though she couldn't hear him through the plugs, or see him through the blindfold, Rae was aware of Sam moving behind her and placing something on the ground between her spread legs. Suddenly she felt the steady, thrumming vibration of something against her clit. The head of whatever was touching her was soft and spongy, alive with electric current as it teased and titillated her sex.

The vibration moved its way through to the plug in her ass, heightening the sensations moving through her sex. She could feel her ass and hips jiggling and twitching of their own accord, while the rest of her remained still, held down with rope, silenced, blinded and gagged.

Without choice or conscious decision, she found herself completely focused on and absorbed by what was happening to her body. There were no distractions and no room for thought.

When the soft, pulsing at her pussy shifted into a higher, faster vibration, Rae gave up the fight, giving in completely to the full feeling in her ass, coupled with the steady tease of her cunt. *Oh god, oh fuck, oh god...* The words played through her brain like a mantra, an accompaniment to the ravaging of her senses by the relentless vibrator rising to a crescendo between her legs.

Just as Rae began to come, a sudden line of fire arced its way across her back. She jerked hard in shock, but the orgasm was too relentless to be stopped by mere pain. As she rode the wave of her release, there was another stroke, and another, slicing along her ass, biting her thighs, stinging her shoulders. The cut of the whip curled around the aching ecstasy of the powerful orgasm, blending in a confusion of pleasure and pain.

Rae screamed against her gag, a muffled, gurgling sound trapped by the rubber ball filling her mouth. Tears wet the back of the sleep mask and sweat slicked her body. She felt the vibrator being shifted at her sex, the direct pressure removed from her clit as the head was now placed higher on her spread pussy. The result was a slow, steady, but easier to tolerate, thrum beneath the constant flicking bursts of pain drawn over her skin in stinging lines from shoulder to calf.

I can't, I can't, I can't...please, no, no, oh...

Her mind began to empty, thoughts sliding out like water sluicing from a glass, leaving an emptiness, a curious kind of peace that comes with total surrender.

Her muscles gave up, her fingers easing their grip against the metal legs of the sawhorse, her body melting onto the leather padding as if her very bones had turned to jelly. Though the whipping continued, along with the steady humming pulse at her cunt, Rae had lost not only the will, but the desire, to fight.

She gave in completely, sliding along a river of pure sensation, her brain no longer distinguishing between pleasure and pain, between fear and desire. She just — was. She existed entirely inside this world of red hot fire and pure white heat, her body jerking spasmodically as orgasm after orgasm was pulled from her, bringing to life the limp ragdoll of her body for as long as it took to come, and to come, and to come again...

~*~

Sam dropped the whip and removed the vibrator apparatus from between Rae's legs. Gripping the base of the butt plug, he eased it from Rae's body, carrying it to the bathroom sink for later cleaning. He unbuttoned his shirt as he came back into the room, letting it fall from his shoulders. He kicked off his boots and socks, and rolled the soft leather pants down his legs.

He stroked his cock a moment as he gazed at her perfect body. Her skin was soft as pressed satin, now beautifully marked with his whip. And that cunt — so responsive, twitching and swollen, the moisture seeping out, its honey scent intoxicating in his nostrils.

I knew it, a voice whispered triumphantly inside his head. Despite her fear, the powerful reaction to what she'd just endured confirmed Sam's initial assessment of her all those months before when they'd made love. She was, beneath the layers of denial and resistance, born for this.

He knew too, that despite his having couched the scene as punishment, it was more than that. Much more. He'd turned the key in the lock of her submission. Over these next thirty days he would open the door. Whether or not she chose to step out of the confines of her carefully constructed world—designed to keep her most deep-seated desires and needs hidden—in the end, that would be up to her.

Jesus god, I want her. I want all of her.

The admission was nothing new, but he understood he wanted her for more than just a month's enforced play. He wanted her to give herself to him, not because she had no choice, but because she wanted what he offered, because she wanted *him*.

Even as he admitted this, he knew the odds were a thousand to one. He'd taken her by force, leaving her no choice but to accept his terms or find herself in prison. She would hate him for this. She would run as fast and as far as she could, the moment he let her go. Was a month of unbridled pleasure and control worth losing her forever?

Or was there another way? Could he somehow take her over to such a degree that she truly became his slave girl? Living only to serve and please him, all thought of her former life and misguided rejection of what he offered buried and forgotten? Could he reduce and control her world to such a degree that she lost sense of time and the outside world, content to stay in his dungeon forever?

Sam shook his head, aware he was treading on dangerous ethical ground. He pushed the strange forbidden thoughts away. He would punish her, yes, and then he would let her go. As they'd agreed.

He continued to gaze at the lovely woman, splayed and bound for his pleasure, his for the taking. He stroked his shaft, several hard tugs to ease the pressure in his aching balls. He leaned over her back, reaching to unbuckle the ball gag and pull it gently from between her lips.

Rae swallowed and then moaned softly, a breathy sweet sound. Her body was wet with sweat beneath him, hot to the touch. As he stared at the crisscross of red welts he'd inflicted on her soft, perfect skin, his cock surged.

Standing upright, he grabbed it, guiding it toward her cunt. He hadn't planned to fuck her, not yet, not the first night. His cock was to be a gift, something she earned. But he couldn't help it. He had to have her, and after all, she was his slave, his cunt, to do with as he wished.

He gripped her hips as he guided himself into her. He moaned, a guttural sound pulled from deep inside him as her velvet wet heat enveloped him. Usually able to pace his pleasure to make it last, this time Sam could no more control his body than she'd been able to against the onslaught of the Hitachi wand he'd placed in its stand between her legs.

She was perfection.

"Rae," he whispered raggedly before getting a hold of himself. Shutting down his mind, he let his body take over, surrendering fully to the tight, hot grip of her cunt. After only a few strokes, he felt the climax surging up through his balls, sliding along his shaft and erupting in spasms of hot, aching pleasure inside her.

He allowed himself a few moments of rest before pulling his spent cock from her warmth. He needed to get her off the sawhorse. She'd been tied down long enough for her first time. Rae groaned and whimpered as he removed the earplugs and the sleep mask and then quickly untied the rope, unwinding it from her wrists and ankles.

He lifted her limp body into his arms. Her eyes were closed, her mouth slack, the lips parted. He held her close as he carried her to the bed in the corner of the dungeon. Gently, he lay her down against the soft sheets. She winced slightly as her abraded skin made contact, but kept her eyes closed.

Same went to the bathroom and returned with a glass of water and a cool, wet washcloth, which he dabbed against her face and neck. He smoothed back the tumble of her tangled hair. Her dark lashes shadowed her flushed cheeks.

Sam felt almost tender toward his slave girl, nearly forgetting she'd been lying to him and stealing from him for months. "Rae," he said in a quiet voice, though it was clearly a command. "Open your eyes. Look at me."

After a beat her eyelids fluttered and then slowly opened. Her pupils were dilated and unfocused. He reached for the glass that he'd set on the nightstand beside the bed and held it near her. "Are you thirsty?"

Rae turned her head toward the glass, her eyes focusing. Her tongue moved over her lips and she nodded, though she made no effort to reach for it. Sam sat beside her and put his arm beneath her shoulders, cradling her as he helped her into a sitting position. She leaned heavily against him.

A part of him knew he had taken her too far, too fast, but he pushed the idea from his mind. She'd needed this — it was her crash course in submission. After all, they only had thirty days.

"Drink." He lifted the glass to her lips, tipping it carefully, letting her take her fill. She drank until the glass was empty and then sagged back against his arm, closing her eyes.

"Are you hungry?"

She nodded, eyes still closed.

"I'll bring your dinner."

Sam eased his arm from beneath her shoulders, letting her head fall to the pillow. He stared down at her a moment. She was breathing easily, and her face was less flushed. She was fine.

He grabbed his leather pants and pulled them on, not bothering with his shirt or boots. He went quickly to the kitchen, taking the plate he'd prepared for her and left in the oven to keep warm. He poured a glass of wine and put the food and drink on a tray, along with a napkin.

Rae lay as he'd left her. Her eyes were closed and her chest rose and fell in a deep, even cadence. He set the tray down on the nightstand and stared down at the sleeping girl, drinking in the lovely curves of her body.

He regarded the neat, dark triangle of pubic hair at her sex. He would shave it so he could better see and access the soft, rising mound of female flesh beneath it. The image made his cock stir but he ignored it—tomorrow was a new day.

"Ready to eat?" he queried.

Rae opened her eyes, turning her head toward the tray. "Yes," she replied in a low voice. She lifted herself higher onto the pillows, wincing slightly as she moved. Her eyes remained on the food, her tongue flicking over her lips.

Sam sat beside her on the bed and took the plate from the tray, balancing it on his knees. He nodded toward the plate. "I even cut the corn off the cob for you." He cut a piece of steak and speared it with the fork. He lifted it to her lips. "Here you go."

"I can—"

"Unh uh," Sam cut her off.

He saw she realized what she'd done—speaking out of turn. "Oh!" she gasped. "Please, um, may I have permission to speak?"

Sam regarded her, amused. At least she was trying. "Yes."

"Could I feed myself?"

"No."

He watched the frustration moving its way over her features, no doubt fighting with the very real hunger she must be feeling. Hunger won out. Rae opened her mouth, her eyes meeting his for a second before sliding away. He let her take the morsel, watching her chew and swallow.

Sam fed her, lifting the wine glass to her lips between bites. When the plate was clean and the wine glass empty, he asked, "Had enough?"

Rae nodded and Sam decided it was time to add a little structure to her responses. "Kneel up on the carpet, Rae," he instructed.

He heard the small, exasperated sigh but let it pass. He waited patiently as she lifted herself from the bed and knelt in front of him. "Hands behind your head," he reminded her. "Knees apart. Show me that cunt."

A pretty blush rose over her cheeks, rather amusing in the circumstances, but also curiously touching. Sam had to remind himself she was a liar and a thief as he stared down at her. "Going forward," he informed her, "you will address me as Sir. You will continue to speak only in response to a direct question, except when asking for permission to speak. Are we clear on this?"

"Yes...*Sir*."

Sam caught the pause and the emphasis on the word, aware of the insolence still lingering in her tone and the anger alive in the sudden flash of fire in her eyes. He smiled, shaking his head. For this month at least, he would wipe all trace of insolence and anger from her, leaving only the passion. She would learn *true* submission. She would come not only to accept, but to embrace what he gave her.

He would see to it.

Chapter 5

Rae awoke with a start and sat bolt upright in her bed. The sudden tug against her throat made her cough and sputter. She fell back against the pillow, her hands fumbling at the collar. She couldn't remove it when it was locked to the chain, not that she would dare anyway.

She lay still, letting the dark dreams ebb away and willing herself to calm down. She reached for the sheets, which had twisted around her legs, pulling them up to her chin. "You're okay," she murmured to herself.

She turned toward the baby monitor that sat beside her on the nightstand. Was he listening, even now? Her hand twitched with the desire to smash the monitor, to hurl it across the room, but she didn't touch it, too afraid of what might happen if she did.

There was a light glimmering from the bathroom, the door of which had been left ajar. Rae ran her hands through her hair, pushing it back from her face. She closed her eyes, imagining the hot, refreshing water of the shower streaming over her, fresh, sweet smelling soap washing away the sweat and grime, cleansing her of his touch.

His touch…

Letting her legs fall open, Rae moved her fingers lightly over the folds of her pussy. She felt the faint throb of her clit as her fingers grazed its hood. When he'd left her last night, he'd told her she wasn't to touch herself when she was alone. Her cunt, he'd crudely said, belonged to him. Who the fuck did he think he was? It was her body to do with as she liked. It was none of his fucking business what she did when she was alone. And anyway, how would he know...

Having spent a night of restless sleep, with lots of time to ponder the situation, Rae had to admit that yesterday had been terrifying and thrilling all at once. He'd done things to her she would never have allowed, never have dreamed she would want, and yet... And yet she couldn't deny her own powerful reaction.

It confused and upset her to think her body had betrayed her as it had—coming so hard and so often while being tortured and abused. What was wrong with her? She was a free-thinking, independent woman. She wasn't some doormat to be used and fucked when it suited a man. She wasn't an object to be degraded, tied down and humiliated for a man's amusement.

In every relationship she'd been in, she'd been the one in control, the one who called the shots, and that suited her. It meshed with her concept of herself as a powerful, competent and liberated woman. She was no shrinking flower, kneeling at the feet of some *man*. On the contrary, Rae Johansen didn't need a man to feel complete.

Her relationships never lasted much longer than a few months—invariably she would get bored with the guy, irritated by his bad habits, annoyed with his neediness or his failure to properly appreciate her. She was always the one to end things, aware when it was time to cut her losses and move on to greener pastures. There were plenty of men eager for her attention and she was in no hurry to settle down with just one.

Sure, it would have been nice in theory to fall in love, to have someone love her, but was there even such a thing as romantic love? She thought about her married friends, all of them disillusioned in some way by their relationship. What they'd sworn was true love all too often seemed to settle into barely tolerating one another, miserable and lonelier together than when they'd been on their own. People just hooked up so they wouldn't be alone. Love was an illusion, a fairytale. People used each other to get what they needed and when it didn't work out, they moved on. It was cleaner that way, and more honest. That's how she'd always done it, and so far it had worked just fine, thank you.

After he'd fed her, Sam had allowed her to wash her face and brush her teeth, but had refused her request for a shower. "In the morning," he'd said. "You'll be properly groomed in the morning." She hadn't liked the sound of that, but she had been too exhausted and frightened by the long, arduous day to question him, even if she'd dared.

He'd locked her collar to a long chain that was bolted into the headboard and had the gall to tell her to "sleep tight". He'd showed her the urinal under the bed to use if she needed to during the night and then he'd left her there, all alone, chained to the bed like a prisoner.

Thirty days...

Somehow she'd slept and was reasonably sure it was now morning. So she'd made it through the first day. Twenty-nine left. Could she really endure being this man's prisoner for that long? Rae shivered, wrapping her arms around herself. Why had she agreed to this bizarre arrangement? Would he keep his word at the end?

She thought of the agreement they'd drafted that would indemnify her of all wrongdoing, going over the wording in her mind. It still left her on the hook to pay back what she'd taken. She'd underestimated him, she realized that now. She'd gotten careless, overconfident as her scheme continued to work, month after month. She'd almost gotten away with it too — that was the infuriating thing. She'd only needed a little more time, a little more money.

She was just *borrowing* the money, after all. She'd always planned to pay the company back, some day. She'd been in a tight spot and she was nothing if not resourceful. She'd done what she needed to in order to stay afloat. And after all, didn't she deserve the funds? She was the one who'd saved him from himself. He'd been so wrapped up in his software code and the miracle of his own genius, he'd lost focus on marketing and finance. She'd saved his damn company, and what gratitude had he shown? Instead of bringing her onboard as a full-fledged partner as he'd promised, he'd let her continue to work as his *assistant*, a hired hand with no direct stake in the business.

And now what was she? She'd voluntarily consented to be his slave, his property, for the next month! She was naked and chained in his basement and not a soul other than Sam knew where she was...

What if he never let her go?

Rae stiffened, her ears perked toward the sound of the basement door opening at the top of the stairs. The overhead light flicked on and Rae squinted against the sudden brightness. She heard Sam's soft but heavy tread on the carpeted stairs. She watched him come into view but she didn't move. As he approached the bed, she shut her eyes. She opened them just a slit, just enough to see his form through the latticework of her lashes.

He was shirtless, dressed in loose-fitting pajama bottoms, his feet bare. He sat on the bed beside her, his weight making the mattress shift. She held her body stiff to keep from rolling toward him.

"Good morning, Rae," he said softly. He stroked her cheek, his touch light on her skin. Despite her rage toward him, and her fear, Rae couldn't deny the sudden pulse at her sex his touch caused. What was wrong with her? She *hated* this man.

"Wake up."

His voice remained soft, but there was command beneath it. She let her lids flutter open and looked at him, saying nothing. He reached for her sheet and she clutched it instinctively to stop him, but he simply pried her fingers from the fabric and pulled the sheet away.

"Turn over. I want to inspect the welts."

Welts! Rae rolled over on the bed, feeling the heat of a blush on her cheeks as he ran his fingers over her back and ass. Her skin tingled to his touch and then, when his hand moved over her right thigh, she winced with pain.

"Nice," he pronounced. "You have some lovely marks this morning. You should be proud."

Proud? Proud he'd whipped her to the point of marking her? Rae was glad her face was averted so he wouldn't see the scowl of furious indignation his words provoked.

He pulled at her shoulder, rolling her onto her back. "Time for a shower." As he spoke, he pulled a key ring from his pajama pants pocket and inserted a small key into the padlock that held the chain in place at Rae's collar.

He led Rae to the bathroom and turned on the water in the shower stall. She stood, waiting for him to leave. Instead he closed the toilet lid and sat down on it. "I—" Rae began, before catching herself. "May I speak?" she forced herself to say instead.

Sam smiled. "Yes."

"I, uh, I need to use the bathroom." *So get the fuck out of here.*

"You can pee in the shower," he said, not moving.

Rae crossed her arms over her chest. "I need to use the toilet," she said, her intestines suddenly cramping.

Sam lifted an eyebrow. "I see," he said. He stood, lifting the toilet lid and gesturing with a hand for her to sit. "Go ahead then."

Rae waited for him to leave, but he just leaned against the sink, watching her with an amused expression. "I need privacy," she finally blurted.

Sam laughed, shaking his head. "Slaves don't get *privacy*, silly girl. In fact, this is a perfect lesson for you. I should have thought it myself. Sit your sweet little ass down on the toilet and do your business. You have nothing to hide in front of me. Nothing. So hurry up, or I might change my mind."

For the second time that morning Rae felt her face heating with embarrassment, while anger boiled in her gut. Her intestines cramped again and his threat lingered in the air between them. Reluctantly she sat on the toilet and willed her body to relax enough for her to move her bowels in front of Sam. She closed her eyes, telling herself it was no big deal. After all, after yesterday what was left to hide? If he got his rocks off by watching a woman take a dump, well, it just confirmed what a sick bastard he was.

She managed to go at last, wiping herself quickly and reaching back to flush the toilet. She stood, closing the toilet lid, averting her eyes from Sam's penetrating gaze and his superior, obnoxious smile.

"Lift your hair and turn around so I can take off your collar," Sam ordered. "Remember, you are never, ever to take it off yourself. If I ever find it off, I'll lock it in place." Rae didn't reply, since no question had been asked. She merely turned as instructed, gathered her hair into a makeshift bun and let him unbuckle the collar, which he set down on the counter beside the sink.

Sam held open the shower door and then took his place again on the toilet seat, his eyes fixed on the clear glass of the stall. Trying to block his presence from her mind, Rae lifted her face into the hot, delicious spray. He'd allowed her to bring her own soap and shampoo when she'd packed her things, and she supposed she should be grateful for that small comfort.

She shampooed her hair twice, letting the hot, soapy water sluice over her body as she rinsed. She squeezed a dollop of conditioner into her palm and pulled it through her hair before taking the bar of soap and lathering it over her skin.

Her next step in a normal shower routine would be to shave her underarms and legs, but there was no razor in the shower and she realized she hadn't packed hers. Suddenly she recalled his statement the night before about her being "properly groomed" in the morning.

She glanced sidelong at him. He was watching her, one hand resting lightly over his crotch, the other stroking his chin. She turned her back to him, lifting her face again into the shower spray, not yet ready to think about what proper grooming might mean.

"Turn off the water and step out."

Reluctantly, Rae did as she was told. She stepped, dripping, onto the bathmat. There was a pile of towels on the counter beside the sink. Sam stood and handed her one. "Wrap your hair. Then stand at attention, hands behind your head. I'll dry your body."

Rae started to retort that she'd dry herself, thank you, but her words died on her lips as her gaze met his. She bent forward, catching her wet hair in the towel and winding it around her head. She straightened, goose bumps rising on her wet skin. Sam moved toward her, his gaze shifting into a glower. "Position," he snapped.

Rae put her hands behind her head, hating him anew. Sam rubbed the towel over her skin, drying her body and limbs with the soft terrycloth. He drew the towel between her legs and beneath her breasts while she stood, stiff and awkward with her fingers laced behind her neck.

When he was done, he picked up the collar. "Arms at your sides," he ordered, again buckling the collar into place around her neck. He took another towel from the counter and spread it over the bathmat. "Lie down on that towel while I get things ready."

Without waiting to see if she obeyed, Sam turned toward the sink and opened the cabinet beneath it. He pulled out a large plastic bowl and a black leather shaving kit, from which he took out a razor, a small plastic bottle of baby oil and a tube of shaving cream. Turning on the tap, he ran it until steam rose and then filled the bowl, squeezing some of the oil in before setting it on the floor beside Rae. He reached for a washcloth and dropped that into the water as well.

Rae was lying on the towel, jittery with nervous anticipation. What was his plan? How did he expect her to shave lying down? Why the fuck had he waited until she was out of the shower to give her a razor?

"Please, Sam, uh, Sir," she began. "May I speak?" Jesus, it felt stupid and humiliating to have to request permission just to speak. Of course, that was his plan, to make her feel like shit. God, she hated him.

"Yes," he said after a beat. "What is it?"

"It's just, I can shave better standing up. It would have made more sense if I'd shaved in the shower. I—"

"I'll be shaving you. Your job is to lie there and keep quiet. We'll do your underarms first."

Rae sat up, the blood in her veins suddenly running cold. "No. Oh no. You can't shave me. I'll do it."

Sam's eyebrows furrowed into a V over his eyes, which grew dark. "Excuse me," he said quietly. "Are you saying *no* to me? A slave does not say *no*, Rae. A slave does what she's told. You've just earned your first punishment of the day, little girl. Knowing you, it won't be your last."

Rae shook her head, aware she was treading on dangerous ground but unable to stop herself. "You might cut me! Please," she pleaded. "Let me do it. Please." She heard the quaver in her voice. No way was she going to let this man near her with a razor! She hugged herself, her lips pressed into a hard, determined line, barely managing to hold her panic at bay.

"Rae, listen to me." Sam's voice was firm. "This isn't up for negotiation. Every morning I'm going to groom you, do you understand? I'm going to shave your underarms, your legs and your cunt. Every morning. You can either lie down and offer yourself to me, or I'll tie you down and do it by force. Do you understand?"

Mutely, Rae shook her head. A tear rolled down her cheek. Sam reached out, tracing its track with his thumb. "You're afraid of being cut?"

She started to nod, then shook her head, afraid to admit it, afraid to let him know of her vulnerability. The sight of her own blood terrified her.

"It's okay." Sam crouched in front of her and cupped her shoulders in his big hands, his voice surprisingly gentle. "I'm not going to cut you, Rae. Trust me, this isn't the first time I've shaved a woman. I know what I'm doing and I won't hurt you. But this *is* going to happen. This morning and every morning that you're with me. We can do it the easy way, or we can make it just as hard as you like."

Rae bit her lip, his words whirling through her brain. Something in his tone made her know there was no negotiating this one. She wasn't going to get out of this, no matter how scared she was. At least she still had some control, in that she wasn't tied down.

He pressed against her shoulder and Rae let herself be pushed back against the towel, though her heart thumped like a bird beating its wings against a closed window. Even though she was lying down, she felt dizzy and a little sick to her stomach. She closed her eyes against the dizziness. Was it possible to faint lying down?

"Relax," she heard Sam say. "Take a deep breath. Go on, breathe. Hold it for three seconds and let it out. Deep breaths."

Rae forced herself to draw in more air, to slow her ragged breathing. She counted to three and exhaled. "That's better," she heard him say. "Again." In and out she breathed, counting and exhaling, willing herself to relax. She kept her eyes closed, soothed in spite of herself by the sound of his voice, deep and gentle. "Breathe. Yes, that's good. Again."

After a while, she did feel calmer. Her heart had slowed to a beat closer to normal and she didn't feel so dizzy. "Much better," Sam said. "I'm going to do your underarms first. You just stay still and you'll be fine."

She didn't resist when she felt him lifting her arms over her head, stretching them out on the bathroom tile. She startled when the warm washcloth moved over her left armpit. "It's okay," Sam said. "You're doing fine." He rubbed some of the shaving cream into her skin.

~ 87 ~

"Now, stay still. I'm going to use the razor. I promise not to hurt you."

She felt the cool blades drawing over her skin in smooth, even lines, and then the washcloth again, warm and soft. He did the other underarm and then patted them both dry. "Not so bad, eh?"

Rae opened her eyes. Sam was smiling at her and she almost smiled back. Instead she closed her eyes again, turning her face away. "Legs next," she heard him say. "Put your feet flat on the floor, knees wide."

The razor moved in slow, careful strokes up and down her calves, followed by his fingers. Again he patted her dry. "Lift your hips," he ordered. "I'm going to put a folded towel under you so I have better access to your pretty little cunt."

Rae thought about refusing. Shaving hadn't been part of their bargain, at least not in her mind. But as she thought over the terms of their peculiar agreement, they had been absurdly vague. His words played in her head. *You'll be my sex slave. My toy to do with as I will. You'll serve your time naked and chained.*

Still reeling from the shock of his catching her out, she hadn't exactly had the leverage or been in the frame of mind to insist on a specific contract for her "punishment" as he'd termed it. And wasn't it better to be lying here, clean and relatively safe, rather than locked in some prison for god knew how long? At least this stint was brief, in the scheme of things. She would get through these few weeks and then she'd move out of New York and put Sam Ryker out of her mind forever.

Sam placed a folded towel under her butt and pushed at her knees, forcing her legs farther apart. He took a pair of small barbers' scissors from the shaving kit and carefully trimmed her pubic hair. Rae bit her lip and clenched her fists, trying to keep perfectly still as the sharp scissors snipped close to her skin.

When he was done, Sam draped the warm, wet washcloth over her pussy. He pressed his palm over her vulva and moved it in a slow, sensual circle that, in spite of her fear at what was to come, felt good. After a moment, he removed the washcloth.

He squirted baby oil onto his fingers and more directly onto her pubic mound. He ran his lubricated fingers gently over her outer labia, coating them with the soft oil. He picked up the razor and Rae's eyes widened, her chest tightening with apprehension.

"This is a real trigger for you, isn't it?" Sam spoke in a musing tone, and she got the feeling he didn't really expect an answer. "We'll have to explore that more," he added, still as if to himself. He looked at her directly, adding, "I'm going to shave your cunt now, slave. Stay still and relax."

Rae had no choice but to comply. She closed her eyes again, trying to let her mind drift away, but her every nerve and muscle was strained as he ran the sharp silver blades again and again over her mons and labia until she was smooth as a baby.

Again he draped the soft, wet washcloth over her skin, pressing his palm against her clit. He removed the cloth and ran his fingers over her denuded sex. "Perfect," he said softly. "Now you're properly groomed, slave girl." He stood and reached an arm down, holding out his hand to her.

"Come on. Up you go. It's time for your training session. But first, your punishment."

Chapter 6

"Put this on." Sam held out the black leather corset, unhooked and unlaced. Rae stared at it as if she'd never seen one before. He'd had her remove the towel and her hair hung wet and loose to her shoulders. She took the corset uncertainly and held it in her hands, her expression one of confusion and distaste.

"Raise your arms. I'll put it on you." He dared her with his eyes to refuse. As she handed back the corset, she met his gaze but then looked away. Slowly she lifted her arms. He secured the corset around her narrow torso, forcing her full breasts up over the top. He hooked it along her side, cinching in her already slender waist. He pulled the leather laces in the back, tightening it still further.

"I can barely breathe," Rae gasped.

"Did I ask you a question?" Sam replied tersely.

"No...Sir," she muttered, barely bothering to disguise her frustration.

He raised his eyebrows. "I'm beginning to think you like to be punished, Rae. How else do we explain your constant breaking of the most basic rules? Perhaps a full day with a ball gag in your mouth will remind you of the very simple rule of keeping your mouth shut, hmm?" She didn't answer, but he recognized the question could be interpreted as rhetorical and let it pass.

He moved in front of her and pointed toward the five-inch heels he'd set down by her feet. "Step into these," he ordered. He watched as she eyed the stilettos dubiously before inserting her pretty feet into them. They were a perfect fit, forcing her into a Barbie Doll arch and accentuating the line of her long, lovely legs. She tottered slightly but managed to find her balance.

He let his eyes travel slowly up her body, lingering hungrily on the bare cunt, gliding over the soft, black leather that hugged her lithe curves, resting on the creamy white breasts jutting over the top of the bustier, the dark pink nipples perking invitingly toward him.

"You look like a perfect whore," he commented, pleased and amused as the color stained her cheeks and throat. He'd never seen her blush during their daily interactions, but since she'd come to his dungeon, she seemed to blush as easily as a schoolgirl.

"So, whore," he continued, savoring his power. "Your punishment this morning is to stand between these two walls." He led her to a corner of the dungeon. Just beside her was a stool, upon which sat an egg timer. "You will keep your nose pressed in the corner, like so." He directed her head until her nose touched the seam of the adjoining walls, "and your hands up like this." He lifted her arms, pressing her palms flat against the walls on either side of her head.

"Spread your legs wide." He kicked lightly at her left ankle with his bare foot, and then at her right until he was satisfied with her stance. "Now, stick out your ass and, no matter what I do to you, you better maintain your position, nose and palms against the wall, ass out."

He reached for the timer and turned the dial to five minutes. It began to tick off the seconds. It was, he knew, in her line of vision. "Your punishment lasts only until the timer rings. But if you fuck up," he warned her, "we start over, got it?"

"Oh, Sam! I—"

Sam reached for the back of her neck and gripped hard. "I said, got it? That's a yes or no question, Rae." He squeezed tighter.

"Yes...Sir," she said in a tiny voice. He let her go and stepped back, stroking his cock through the thin fabric of his pajamas as he admired the full round globes of her small but perfect ass beneath the tight leather binding of the corset.

Soon he would have her at his feet, his cock stuffed down that pretty throat. But not yet...she hadn't earned it yet. Instead he went to the toy cabinet and returned with a riding crop, its long rectangle of red leather pretty against her pale skin. He smacked her right ass cheek lightly, watching the supple flesh jiggle in response. She kept her position. He smacked the other cheek, quite a bit harder. She gasped but still stayed in place. Good girl.

He licked his right index finger and reached between her legs, pressing the digit into her softness. She grunted and shuddered but, to her credit, still kept her palms pressed flat, her nose to the wall. He moved his finger inside her, savoring the hot clamp of muscle and the moistening flesh. She could protest all she liked — her cunt didn't lie.

He smiled cruelly and pulled his finger from her, reaching to cup her mons from behind. He pushed his palm against her, moving in a slow, grinding circle over her spread pussy. He stepped closer, reaching around her to find and roll a nipple between his fingers, enjoying its swell as it hardened beneath his touch. He bent and kissed her shoulder, biting lightly, just a nudge of his teeth to let her know his power. She shuddered again, arching against his palm, but otherwise remained still and quiet.

Stepping back, he lifted the crop again, letting its working end land with several sharp cracks against her bottom. He cropped her steadily, methodically covering her ass and thighs. He saw she was clenching her hands, the palms no longer flat against the wall.

"Palms flat," he reminded her. "We start again." He waited until she uncurled her fingers and pressed her hands again against the wall. She shifted a little on her heels. Her feet were probably tired by now. When she was still and once again in proper position, he reset the timer.

Sam wasn't one of those men with a particular fetish for stiletto heels and corsets, though he had to admit they did create a lovely picture. But for him, it was more about the punishment — the confining of his slave in apparel that restricted and limited her, reminding her of her place and position. The fact that Rae looked gorgeous in the outfit was just an added perk.

Sam slapped at her thighs and calves with the crop. She yelped and pressed herself into the corner, as if she could get away from the stinging leather. He struck her ass, alternating between cheeks, watching the skin redden.

Stepping back, he aimed carefully and smacked her between the legs, catching her delicate labia with a satisfying thwack. Rae screamed and jerked her legs closed, reaching down with one hand to cup her cunt.

Sam smiled behind her, having expected this. "Oh dear," he said with mock sympathy. "You seem to have fallen out of position. I guess we'll just have to start over." Again he set the timer for five minutes, waiting patiently while Rae resumed the proper stance. She had begun to whimper and her legs were shaking, but she placed her palms flat against the wall and again buried her nose in the corner.

Sam couldn't help but stroke his cock, hard as bone beneath his pajamas. If she'd been his lover he'd have fucked her then and there, pressing her against the wall, impaling her from behind with his cock.

Instead he forced himself under control, and gave her fifty swats on each cheek. She stayed in position, though she continued to whimper and shake. Three minutes left.

He stepped back again, watching her. Reaching between her legs, he stroked her labia, flicking the bud of her clit with a light but persistent touch. He felt a tremor move through her body. He pressed two fingers into her wet heat.

She expelled a sudden breath and stifled a small moan. He withdrew his fingers and used them, now slick with her own juices, to rub and tease her erect clit, moving in concentric circles over her cunt until she began to tremble in earnest, small breathy cries signaling an impending climax. He knew he could send her tumbling into an orgasm with just a few more strokes.

The timer dinged.

Sam dropped his hand and stepped back.

"Punishment's over."

~*~

It took Rae several seconds to realize what had happened. She'd been on the edge of a powerful orgasm, ready to slide over, in spite of her stinging flesh, in spite of her awkward position and aching feet. Why had he stopped? She wanted to beg him to continue, to let her come, but she snapped her mouth shut before any words slipped out. She'd be damned if she gave him the satisfaction. Instead she let her arms fall slowly to her sides. She turned back, keeping her expression as neutral as she could while she struggled to catch her breath.

"Please, Sir," she ventured, "may I speak?"

He nodded, cocking one eyebrow with ironic amusement. Jesus, she wanted to smack his face. Instead she said, "May I take off the heels? They're hurting me."

Again he nodded and she bent down to reach for the shoes, barely able to move in the constricting corset. Giving up, instead she managed to push them off by using the toes of one foot against the heel of the other. She ignored her throbbing cunt, focusing instead on the relief as she flexed her toes.

She didn't understand it, but somehow Sam was able to drag these incredible, huge orgasms from her, climaxes so powerful she couldn't resist them, even if she'd wanted to. What the fuck was that about?

With most men, most of the time, Rae faked orgasm. It was easier than having to work for it, and men were so easy to fool. A few moans and sighs, some rapid breathing, a sudden tensing of the body and then..."Oh, John (Hank, Robert, Jake, fill in the blank here), that was sooo good. Oh, you are the best..."

They would puff with pride, preening at what they fancied was their unique ability to really satisfy a woman. She would wait until later, once they'd gone home, or she'd left their place and returned to her own bed, to take her pleasure.

In point of fact, Sam was one of the few men who had made her come—she hadn't had to fake a thing. What was it about him? Surely it wasn't the rope and chain and the arrogant swagger? At the time, she'd chalked it up to her being especially horny that particular night, so horny she'd managed to come in spite of his weird kinks.

But if that were the case, how did she explain her reactions now? Why was her body, usually immune or at least indifferent to a man's touch, so orgasmic, in spite of the horrific things he'd done to her? What the hell was going on? Was she losing her mind?

Sam led her to the bed and she sank gratefully onto the mattress, turning to her side as the sheet chafed her tender ass and thighs. "Lift your arms," Sam said, as he reached for the long line of sturdy hooks that held the corset in place. As they sprang free, Rae heaved a sigh of relief and drew air gratefully into her expanding lungs. Sam rolled the corset and took it, along with the high heels, to the cabinet along the back wall.

Returning to stare down at her, he said, "You rest while I get our breakfast." He turned and walked away, climbing up the stairs. She heard the snick of the lock in the door. Rolling gingerly to her back, she looked down at herself and cupped her shaven pussy, exploring the smooth skin with her fingers.

She'd been so close to a really powerful orgasm when that stupid timer had gone off. Maybe she'd just finish the job herself. She licked her fingers and touched her inner labia, stroking the folds and seeking the hard button of her clit.

Again she recalled his admonishment that she wasn't to touch herself when alone. Well, he shouldn't have denied her that orgasm, then. She needed to come, to take the edge off. Fuck him, anyway. What he didn't know wouldn't hurt him, or rather, her.

She closed her eyes, moaning very softly as she stroked herself. The ache he'd left by stopping her just before she came bloomed at once into a hot, urgent need. She rubbed herself fast, aware she might only have seconds before he came back. She gritted her teeth to keep from making any noise, aware he might be eavesdropping on the stupid baby monitor.

She arched upward into her hand, shuddering in a series of small climaxes that eased the ache, but left her wanting more. Left her wanting the kind of intensity that somehow only Sam was able to give her.

She lay still, legs akimbo, her hand still buried in her cunt, drifting lightly along the edge of consciousness. When she heard his tread on the stairs, she snatched her hand from her pussy and closed her legs, reaching for the sheet.

He entered the room, a tray in hand, the smell of coffee preceding him. Rae pulled herself upright against the pillow and swallowed, suddenly starving. Sam set the tray down on the nightstand. She saw it contained a plate piled high with scrambled eggs and bacon, as well as several slices of buttered toast and two cups of coffee.

"You take yours black, right?"

Rae nodded, surprised he remembered, since she was always the one who brought the coffee when they met at his office. She looked again at the tray, noting there was only one fork. Sam took it and scooped up a large bite of egg, which he placed in his mouth.

Rae's stomach rumbled as she watched him. He looked at her, answering her unspoken question. "You may hold your own coffee cup, but I'll feed you. You haven't yet earned the right to eat by yourself."

Whatever the fuck that means, Rae thought, but she kept her face blank and simply nodded. She reached for the mug, inhaling the moist, scented steam before taking a sip. It was delicious, strong and hot just like she liked it. She took another sip, hungrily eying the crisp bacon and buttered toast.

Sam lifted the fork, laden with egg. Feeling a little ridiculous, but too hungry to worry overmuch, Rae opened her mouth. The eggs were perfectly cooked, fluffy and moist. He followed with a piece of bacon. Eagerly Rae accepted the food, ravenous.

She was surprised at just how good it all tasted. Unlike most women she knew, Rae had never especially cared about food. She never lusted after ice cream, or gorged herself on potato chips and chocolate when she was feeling blue. Food was just fuel, necessary to keep going. In fact, breakfast was usually just coffee, or at most a roll eaten on the run.

But today, for some reason, each bite was a bit of heaven, sheer perfection exploding against her taste buds, satisfying a deep longing she hadn't been aware of. She closed her eyes, savoring the chewy texture of the toast slathered with melted butter. She chewed slowly and licked her lips to catch an errant crumb.

When she opened her eyes, she saw Sam was watching her, that amused, insolent smile again playing over his mouth. "Enjoying it, huh?" he said, the smile sliding into a grin. Something in the way he said it, and the gleam in his eye, embarrassed her, as if she been caught doing something better kept private.

But it was a direct fucking question and so she forced herself to reply. "Yes, thank you, Sir," she said stiffly.

Sam dipped his head toward her. "You're learning, finally, how a proper slave girl speaks."

She said nothing to this, but returned her focus to the plate, silently willing him to feed her more of the delicious food. They continued to eat the rest of the meal in silence, with Sam alternating bites between them. It was a lot of food, especially for someone who never ate breakfast, but when the plate was empty, Rae wanted more.

Sam shifted his weight on the mattress and turned. He pointed toward the wall across from her bed. "See that device up there?" She followed his gaze, focusing on what looked like a small smoke detector, a tiny red light blinking at its center. She nodded.

"That, my dear," Sam said, "is a camera. It's attached to a closed-circuit TV. It's set up with a night vision lens so I can see what you're doing down here, even in the dark."

Rae swallowed hard and bit her lip. Had he...? Before she even finished formulating the thought, Sam provided the answer. "You, Rae Johansen, are a willful, disobedient girl. Admittedly, you've only been here a short while, but you seem incapable of following very basic rules. Did I not tell you that you weren't to touch yourself unless I gave you express permission?"

Rae felt at once hot and cold, embarrassed to realize he'd been spying on her, and frightened at what the consequences were going to be. There was no way out of this one. He was staring her down, waiting for her reply.

"Yes," she managed to croak.

"Yes, what?"

She cleared her throat. "Yes, Sir. I—I guess I forgot."

"I guess you did." His mouth was turned down in a frown, but she could almost swear she saw his eyes sparking with amusement. He was *enjoying* this—of course he was, the sadistic bastard. He liked nothing better than to catch her breaking the fucking *rules*!

"What happens to slave girls who disobey?"

Rae's mouth felt dry. The food she'd eaten lay like lead in her stomach. He was watching her, clearly expecting a reply.

"They get...punished," she whispered.

"That's correct. They do." Sam stood, crossing his strong arms over his bare chest. "Let's see now. The punishment should fit the crime. You can't seem to keep your hands off your cunt, or rather, *my* cunt. And you like to come without permission, taking your pleasure at your own discretion, despite the fact you were expressly forbidden from doing so." He stroked his chin and pursed his lips, staring at the ceiling in a caricature of someone thinking hard.

"I know just what we'll do," he announced, looking down at her. "We'll combine punishment with training." He glanced at his watch. "Damn, I have a few phone calls I have to handle this morning first — you'll have to wait. Since I can't trust you to behave on your own, you'll spend the time while I'm working in your cage."

"Sam, not the —"

"That's it, I've had enough." The sparkle had left his eyes now, leaving only the frown. Leaning down, Sam gripped Rae's arm, hauling her from the bed as she stumbled to keep her footing. "That's the last time you speak out of turn." He gripped her firmly by the shoulders. "Wait right here. Don't move. Not an inch, you understand?"

Terrified, Rae nodded. Tears were pressing at her eyelids. To think, she'd nearly relaxed during breakfast, but now every muscle in her body was tensed with fear and trepidation. What was going to happen?

Sam went to the cabinet and returned a moment later, a roll of duct tape in his hand. He pulled a long strip and ripped it with his teeth. "Close your lips," he said brusquely. "You can't seem to keep your mouth shut, so we'll just shut it for you."

Before she could react, he pressed the sticky tape over her mouth, patting it down around the edges. Grabbing the O ring at the front of her collar, he dragged her toward the cage. Pushing at her shoulders, he forced her to her knees. "Get in."

Rae crawled awkwardly into the confining space, her heart was skittering like a caged mouse. "I'll be watching you, slave, so behave yourself." He clanged the small gate shut and popped the padlock into place.

As he walked away, Rae mewled behind the tape but he ignored her. As the door at the top of the stairs slammed closed, Rae slumped down onto her side, curling in on herself. She shifted so her back was to the camera, though it occurred to her there were probably other cameras placed about the room — she would have to look more carefully when he let her out.

Tentatively, she touched the sticky tape that covered her lips and extended several inches on either side of her mouth. She ached to pull it off but didn't dare. He was angry enough as it was. She lay still, for a while just letting the scattered, panicked thoughts ricochet through her mind. This was only day two. How in the hell was she going to get through this entire month! Everything was so hard and so scary. He punished her at every turn. She thought about this for a long while. The punishments came because she didn't obey the rules. Yes, they were arbitrary and offensive and intrusive, but they were clear. If she could remember to obey his fucking rules, it would be that much easier on her. She drew air in through her nostrils, willing herself to calm down.

If she was going to get through the next twenty-nine days, she needed to change the way she was handling, or rather, not handling things. Sam Ryker was calling the shots. She'd given him this power over her. She needed to accept that and somehow find a way to work with it, to work through it, without losing her mind in the process.

She would approach this as a challenge. Think of it as a trial to be overcome, a series of tests she could either pass or fail. She closed her eyes, mentally ticking off the rules as best she could.

One: Only speak when answering a direct question.

Two: Address him as Sir.

Three: If you need to speak, ask permission first.

Four: Don't touch yourself without express permission.

Five: When you're going to come, ask for permission first.

Six: Do everything he says, without hesitation.

That last one encompassed a lot, but it was straightforward. Just do what he said and stay out of trouble. It was really pretty simple. She was in this for the duration. She needed to get her mind around that and stop resisting it. If she could manage to obey these dictates, it would make her time easier.

You did the crime, now do the time.

It was strange to admit, but until this moment, she hadn't really thought of what she'd done as a crime. She was just *borrowing* the funds, she'd told herself, and had some vague plan of paying it back one day, if not in actual dollars, at least in service and dedication to *Ryker Solutions*.

But that was crazy thinking, she now had to admit to herself. She'd been so caught up in her drama, frightened of the lawsuits that had been threatened and the financial ruin she was facing if she didn't come up with the monies owed that she hadn't really stopped to think about what she was doing. She was a thief. A liar and a thief. She was no better than the unscrupulous assholes who had duped her into the deal in the first place.

It never occurred to you to maybe come to me and ask for help? He'd asked her that when confronting her. The answer, honestly, was no. She hadn't thought of turning to Sam, or indeed to anyone, for help. It would have been an admission of just how badly she'd fucked up.

But she'd only made it worse, by taking the easy way out of her troubles. Now she found herself living out some kind of nightmare, locked in this dungeon, waiting in a cage wearing a dog collar with her mouth taped shut. She was a prisoner, a voluntary slave, at the mercy of a man who held all the cards.

Still, this was better than jail, she reminded herself. It was finite, and thirty days was a lot less than what she'd get if convicted by a court of law. She could do this the easy way, or the hard way. Why make it worse than it had to be?

When he came back, she'd submit to her punishment. What choice did she have? She cradled her hands beneath her cheek and closed her eyes, slipping into an uneasy doze while she waited for Sam's return.

Chapter 7

Sam showered and dressed quickly, not bothering to shave, as he'd decided to work from home while Rae was sequestered in his dungeon. He took care of the few customer calls he couldn't put off, handholding a new client through some programming issues and working out some kinks with the IT guy at *Ichi Products'* American branch. All the time he was on his phone and computer, he kept glancing at the closed-circuit TV screen. He had four cameras placed at various intervals along the ceiling in the dungeon and he'd selected the camera view of the cage so he could keep his eye on Rae.

He knew what he was doing was wrong by conventional standards. The bywords of *safe, sane and consensual*, which were such a mantra in the BDSM community, wouldn't include leaving a sub alone in a cage with her mouth taped shut. But then, he thought with a snort, none of what he was doing would fly if he applied those bywords.

This was beyond the pale, he told himself. It wasn't about BDSM — he was exacting a price for Rae's thievery. He was punishing her for bilking him out of a lot of money. It had nothing to do with D/s.

He knew, even as the thought entered his mind, that he was lying. It had everything to do with it.

Since that one night he'd claimed her, he'd never really gotten over the intensity of her reactions and the spark of pure need and desire he'd seen deep in her eyes. Afterwards, when she'd rejected what he offered with such certainty, he'd known she was lying, not necessarily to him, but to herself. She was afraid to admit she was submissive and a masochist. She thought it made her less of a woman, somehow. She had confused an honest, erotic exchange of power with somehow being made "less than", subjugated and demeaned rather than exalting in her surrender.

And he hadn't been able to reach her. She hadn't given him, or indeed herself, a chance to explore that intensity. It was his fault as much as hers, he knew. He'd rushed her. In his greed and passion for her, he'd move too far, too fast.

But now the game had changed. The rules were all new, and he was the one writing them. He felt electrified with power — it snaked through his blood like a livewire, heightening sensation, making him feel like he could bend steel in his hands or conquer worlds. He knew he was stepping over the line, way over, but who was to stop him?

She'd agreed to the terms. The proof was down in his dungeon. He focused on the screen. She was curled into a fetal ball, her back to the camera. He could see the delicate outline of her spine beneath her smooth skin, the flare of her hips, the luscious curve of her ass.

He hadn't bothered with underwear so it was easy to access his cock by slipping his hand into his jeans. He curled his fingers around the shaft, feeling it swell as he stared at the naked, caged girl waiting for him. He was frustrated with how she'd continued to fight him at every turn, but reminded himself it had only been twenty-four hours since she'd entered his dungeon. He had time, lots of time, to bend and mold her to his will. By the time he was done with her, would she even want to step out of the confines of what would become her world?

Sam shook away this thought, aware he was treading on very thin and dangerous moral ice with what he was doing. He wouldn't think about it now. He'd just take this one day at a time, feeling his way as he punished the thief waiting downstairs for her just desserts.

He opened and booted up her laptop. He typed in her work email user name and password and quickly scanned the inbox for anything that needed immediate attention. He handled what he could and made a few notes to check with her later on. Though he'd made her give him her personal email password too, he decided they would go through it together later. He'd created an away message for her—"I'm traveling on business for the next month, so forgive me if my responses take a while. I'll be in touch!" If there were love letters in there from boyfriends, he didn't want to know about it.

He heard a soft moan in the baby monitor and looked up at the screen. Poor baby, with her mouth taped shut, curled up like a kitten in her cage. Sam stood and adjusted his still-erect cock in his jeans. Time to take care of his slave girl.

~*~

Rae crawled gratefully out of the confining space and knelt back on her haunches, staring up at her captor. He had dressed in a pale gray T-shirt that hugged his broad shoulders and muscled biceps. Golden stubble etched his cheeks and jaw. His jeans hung loose and low on his hips. She could just see the thin line of fine hair that ran from his navel, disappearing beneath his jeans, drawing her eye to the bulge at his crotch. In spite of herself and the situation, she couldn't deny the man was seriously sexy.

He crouched in front of her and stroked her cheek. "If I take off the tape, are you going to be a good girl and follow the rules?"

Rae nodded. She wished he'd let her take the gag off herself but just getting it off was good enough. She tensed as he pulled at a corner of the sticky tape. He pulled slowly, edging his fingers beneath it as he tugged. It hurt a little, but at least he hadn't yanked it. The skin beneath felt tender and itchy, but otherwise no worse for wear.

"Better?" Sam asked.

"Yes, thank you...Sir."

Sam nodded, clearly pleased with her response and Rae felt a curious kind of pride—she'd pleased him. That was good.

"Time for training. You need to pee?"

"Yes, please." She'd felt the urge while in the cage but hadn't wanted to use the urinal, especially now that she knew he might be watching her. He let her use the bathroom without even following her inside. When she was done, she stepped back into the room, at once frightened and curious as to what he had in mind.

She watched as he brought a full-length mirror from a corner of the room. He gestured with his chin toward the bed. "Lie down with your head just below the pillows." Rae obeyed while Sam placed the mirror on the floor at the end of the bed, angling it so she could see herself.

Pushing the pillows aside, he climbed onto the bed behind her, cradling her between his legs. She could see them both now in the mirror, Sam's long, jean-clad legs on either side of her naked body, his firm, muscular chest warm against her back through the thin cotton of his T-shirt. They could have been lovers.

But they weren't. Rae tensed, holding herself stiff against Sam's body. She was his prisoner, held here against her will. *No, stop it. You agreed to the terms. Don't make it harder on yourself than it has to be. Remember the rules. Follow the rules...*

"As a part of your training today," Sam broke into her thoughts, "we'll test your modesty." He lifted her as he spoke and scooted them both down toward the bottom of the bed. "Pull your legs up, feet flat, knees wide. I want to take a good look at your bare cunt."

Rae felt the heat rushing to her face. Whatever she'd been expecting, it hadn't been this. She had never let a man linger too long down there. For all her confidence with her figure and shape, this was one area where she was not comfortable at all. She realized she'd rather be placed in the corner again in those god-awful shoes than have to spread her legs for Sam's unwelcome inspection.

Though she hadn't thought of it in ages, all at once Rae flashed back to her freshman year of high school when she'd been out on her first (and only) date with Danny Hunter, a senior who all the girls were after. She didn't know him well at all, but had been deeply flattered when he'd asked her out. Certain her parents would never let her date a senior, she'd lied, telling them she was going to the movies with her friend, Jean. She'd expected Danny to take her out for pizza or maybe to a party, but instead he'd just driven her to the parking lot of a nearby university and suggested they move from the front to the back of his father's Cadillac, where he produced a small cooler filled with cans of beer.

They sat in the dark, drinking beer and talking about their school's sports teams and Danny's choice of college the upcoming year. Not used to drinking, she'd gotten plenty drunk, plenty fast. She'd been both excited and very nervous when Danny had started making out with her. After all, he was super hot, even if he was moving faster than she was used to with the boys her own age.

His kisses were sloppy but his hands were smooth and fast, unbuttoning her blouse, slipping into her bra, easing the zipper down her jeans. He kept telling her she was so hot, and he wanted her so much. She kept thinking what a great story this would make over lunch on Monday with her girlfriends. They'd be so jealous that Danny Hunter had taken her out! Danny Hunter thought she was hot!

Somehow, he'd managed to get her jeans and panties down when all at once he turned on the ceiling light and leaned down, his face very close to her exposed pussy. Suddenly sober, Rae had tried to slam her legs together, deeply embarrassed at his scrutiny. But Danny had placed his hands on her thighs, forcing them apart.

"Let me look," he'd insisted, his voice slurred with liquor. "I like to see a girl's twat up close and personal. I can tell if she's a virgin or a slut. How 'bout you, babe? You a virgin or a slut? Let me see." He laughed, the sound derisive and insulting in her ears.

She had squirmed away from him, furious and deeply humiliated. "Take me home," she'd insisted, forgetting the movie she was supposedly at wouldn't be over for at least an hour.

He'd acted surprised, and then angry. "I should have known better than to take out a *kid*," he'd snarled, but he'd taken her home, making his tires squeal as he pulled away from the curb.

If only she could insist that Sam take her home. But she wasn't fourteen, she reminded herself. She could do this. She would pass his fucking modesty test, whatever it was. Each minute she got through was one less minute she had to go through, one minute closer to freedom.

"Open your legs," Sam instructed her. "Let me see what's mine." She looked at him in the mirror. He was no longer smiling and his eyes held a curious, dangerous spark. Rae's heart skipped a beat but she didn't dare disobey him. Slowly, she let her legs fall open, keeping her eyes on his face. He placed a large hand on either thigh, holding her open in front of the mirror.

"Don't look at me," he instructed. "Look at your cunt. Tell me what you see."

"What?" Rae felt flustered, unsure of what he was saying.

"Look at your cunt, Rae. Examine it in the mirror. Describe it to me."

"I—I don't know what you mean," she said helplessly, her face beet red.

She tensed, afraid he was going to yell at her, threaten her in some way, but when he spoke, his voice was calm, even patient. "It's a simple task, Rae. I want you to really take a look at your pussy. Tell me what you see. Describe the folds, the color and the shape. Go on. It's not a trick. I really want to know what you see."

She had never, she realized with some surprise, ever really looked at herself down there. Why would she? And why was he making her now? She glanced again at his face and saw the warning there. She swallowed and let her eyes move down toward her splayed sex. It looked strange, so naked without the obscuring cover of pubic curls.

Men seemed to be fascinated with pussies, but at the same time, they were so insulting when they wanted to be. They loved to fuck, sure, but did they regard a woman's sex as beautiful? *Filthy cunt*, *dirty twat*, *slit*, *gash*, *hole*, the joke about the blind man at the fish market saying, "good morning, ladies," — these images and words were as much a part of the American lexicon as home sweet home and apple pie. Women had received mixed messages about their sex all their lives. What did he want from her?

She took a deep breath and let it out slowly. She could do this. She was a grown woman, for god's sake. She was proud of her body. Wasn't she?

She looked down, really seeing her pussy, possibly for the first time in her life. "I see…" she hesitated, still not entirely sure what he wanted. She cleared her throat and tried again. "I see folds of flesh, the outer ones are pink, the inner ones are darker, sort of purple, I guess."

Was this what he wanted? He said nothing but gave her a slight nod of encouragement.

She continued, almost warming to the task. It really wasn't ugly. It was even kind of pretty, in an abstract sort of way. "Um, it looks sort of like a tiger lily, when they aren't open yet before the sun comes up, you know?" She glanced at him, wondering if this was what he wanted.

He nodded again, a whisper of a smile moving over his mouth. "Go on," he urged softly. He reached for her, gently spreading the outer labia. He used one finger to pull back the hood at her center, revealing the tip of her clit, which peeped out like a tiny flower bulb ready to bloom.

"Go on," he said again.

Rae stared down at her clit, which swelled before her eyes as Sam moved his finger with a feathery touch over it and around it. "Gosh," she said, startled. "I've never seen that before. I didn't realize it got big like that when I was…um…aroused."

Sam nodded again. He took her right hand and lifted it to his lips, surprising her by licking her fingers. He then took her wrist, guiding her hand toward her spread pussy.

"Make yourself come for me. Show me how it's done."

Rae swallowed again, her embarrassment resurfacing at the thought of touching herself in front of someone, especially in front of this man, who held her against her will in his dungeon.

And yet, her pussy was throbbing, the folds swollen and moist, her clit pulsing at its center. This was certainly better than a beating, wasn't it? He was asking her to come—what was the big deal? She masturbated all the time when she was alone. She would just close her eyes and—

"Eyes open," Sam snapped. "I want you to watch what you're doing. I want you to pay attention to your body. And when you're about to come, I want you to ask me for permission. Understand?"

She stared in the mirror into his face and then down at her pussy. She had no choice. She was his prisoner, this was beyond her control.

Slowly she reached for her sex with her wet fingers and began to rub in a circular motion around her hooded clit. She dipped her fingers into her pussy, watching as her fingers disappeared and then reemerged, shiny and wet. Again she rubbed herself, her eyes on her sex.

It was harder than she'd expected to keep her eyes open. She was used to closing them and losing herself in a fantasy, usually involving Johnny Depp or Neal Patrick Harris. Instead she forced herself to focus, watching as the folds swelled and darkened. She dared a quick glance at Sam's face, half fearing to see derision or that insolent, knowing smile on his face, but he was focused as intently as she on her sex, his lips lightly parted, his eyes burning with intensity.

She refocused on her bare cunt, bringing her left hand up and slipping a finger inside herself as she continued to rub and swirl the fingers of her right hand over and around her clit. She began to pant, and it took every bit of willpower to keep her eyes from sliding closed of their own accord.

She felt the melting heat of an orgasm roiling just below the surface and remembered just in time to beg, "Please, may I come?"

She struggled against the rising tide of her impending orgasm as she strained for his answer, the fingers of her right hand moving wildly over her sex, her left second and third fingers sliding wetly in and out like pistons.

"Yes."

She let the tide sweep her away.

Chapter 8

He'd held her in the dungeon for five days now, waking her each morning for her shower and grooming, and then subjecting her to a series of erotic torture and training sessions.

She no longer hesitated in addressing him as Sir, and the constant resistance had ebbed away to almost nothing. Sam had abandoned the idea of going into the city to work while she was in his dungeon—he didn't want to leave her alone down there. Fortunately, he had a full computer lab in his home office. The only inconvenience was in meeting new clients, but he didn't have anything going at the moment anyway—the *Ichi* job had absorbed all his time and attention the past few months.

He'd had to consult with Rae on two occasions regarding some financial details in the contract. How strange that had been—Rae naked and imprisoned in his dungeon, leaning over the document and explaining points he needed to understand.

It was early, before seven, though Sam had already been up nearly two hours. He slept very lightly with Rae in the house, waking several times a night to make sure she was okay, and taking a long time to fall back asleep, images of what they'd done that day swirling through his brain and hardening his cock.

Turning away from the computer, he looked at the closed-circuit TV screen. The view was set on camera two—her bed. She looked like a captured angel curled on her side, her hands tucked beneath her cheek, lit by the soft glow of the nightlight. Her sheet had fallen to just below her breasts. He could see the outline of her nipple, jutting sweetly.

Yes, he thought, as he stared at the naked, chained woman, *today I'll introduce her to the pleasure and pain of the clamps.*

Sam turned back toward his computer and clicked on a video he'd downloaded from one of his favorite porn sites. In it a woman not unlike Rae, with dark, flowing hair and pouting lips, was securely bound face down on a high, wide table. Her knees were bent, her arms underneath her between her legs, her wrists tied to her ankles. Her ass was forced up high, the cheeks splayed, nothing left to the imagination. The height of the table was such that her head was level with the erect cock of the naked man standing in front of her. Pulling her head up by the hair, he eased his long, thick shaft into her open mouth, ordering her to swallow it.

Sam hadn't yet dressed that morning. He was wearing his favorite shorts, as the day had already dawned hot and sticky outside. He reached for his cock and pulled it from the button fly, stroking it. Wouldn't it be nice to have his own slave girl kneeling right now between his legs, sucking him off while he watched...

Well, why not?

He hadn't allowed her out of the dungeon since he'd first brought her home. But she was much more compliant now. Maybe she'd earned a trip out of the basement, if just for a little while. Maybe she'd earned the chance to suck his cock.

Sam paused the video and stood, tucking his cock back into his shorts. He glanced at his watch. He usually let Rae sleep until eight but he wanted her *now*. Over the past few days he'd established a routine for her. He would change the channel on the baby monitor so that she could hear him through it, and let her know she had five minutes to present herself.

This meant she was to get out of the bed and kneel up on the floor, legs spread wide, hands behind her head, while she waited for him. He loved to come down the stairs and see her there, naked with her breasts thrust out, her shaven cunt peeking between her legs, her hair tousled around a face still smudged with sleep.

This morning, however, he would wake her himself, in person. He moved quickly down the hall toward the basement door, which he unlocked and pulled open. Grabbing the dungeon key ring from its hook, he stepped lightly down the stairs on bare feet, stopping at the bottom as his eyes adjusted to the dim light.

Rae stirred, turning from her side to her back, her right hand disappearing beneath the sheet. Sam moved quietly across the carpet until he was beside the bed. He gripped the hem of the sheet and pulled it slowly down her naked body. Her hand was cupped over her bare mons, the fingers hidden between her legs.

Sam's cock hardened at the erotic sight. He would have to make her masturbate again for him soon. She'd better not be touching herself now though—even in her sleep—or he'd have to punish her. He watched for a few moments, but her hand was still, and her breathing had deepened again.

He thought about turning on the overhead light, but instead moved toward the bathroom and flicked on the light, opening the door wide to let it brighten the room. When he sat down beside her, Rae's eyes flew open and she jerked her hands toward her mouth.

"Oh, Sir! I didn't hear you! I'm sorry, I must have slept through—"

"Hey, calm down," Sam said gently. "It's okay. It's early. I wanted to wake you myself this morning. I didn't mean to startle you." He gripped her hands and lowered them from her face. She continued to stare at him, but the fear and confusion ebbed slowly away as he stroked her cheek.

Such *power* he held over her! This was more than a dominant lover's sway. He was her lord and master. He decided when she slept, ate, orgasmed. He decided when she'd earned a punishment or a reward. No one in the world but he knew she was imprisoned in his dungeon. If he wanted, he could keep her there forever…

Sam pushed away these thoughts to contemplate later. Rae was searching his face, as if she could read there his plans for her, though she wisely didn't ask. She was learning, slowly but surely.

"How would you like to come upstairs?"

Rae looked puzzled. "What?"

"Upstairs. Out of the dungeon for a while. I have something in my study I want to show you."

"Oh." Rae seemed to be thinking it over, which was kind of funny, since his question wasn't really a choice. She'd do what he said, when he said, end of discussion. Still, he waited until she nodded. "I would like that, Sir."

"Good. Use the bathroom if you want. I'll groom you later."

Rae slid from the bed and hurried toward the bathroom. He didn't follow her, though he sometimes liked to watch her, just to make her blush. He heard the toilet flush and the sound of running water, and a moment later she stood in front of him, shifting uncertainly from foot to foot.

"Is that how you greet me in the mornings?" Sam affected a stern tone. He was pleased to see her sink quickly to her knees. She knelt back on her haunches and spread her legs as she lifted her arms and locked her fingers behind her neck. Such a beauty; he never tired of looking at her. She was staring off into the middle distance, her face closed off and inscrutable, though she couldn't hide the faint blush that had crept over her chest and cheeks as it did every morning when he forced her to expose herself like this for his pleasure.

"Better," he said, extending his hand. "Now follow me. I have a job for you."

~*~

Rae followed Sam uncertainly up the basement steps. She would have liked to stay in bed, but at the same time she was excited at the prospect of going upstairs. He'd said he had a job for her. Was he talking business? Why take her upstairs for that? Every other time he'd consulted with her on some business-related issue, he'd brought it down to her.

She followed him along a hall to a door that he pushed open, revealing a large, sunny room that, like his office downtown, had three computers and lots of clutter. There was a landline telephone. She could grab it and dial 911! They'd come no matter what—she wouldn't even have to say a word.

Even as this scenario played itself out, she rejected it. If she did that, even if kidnapping charges stuck, he'd still have the evidence of her embezzlement, and then he'd be sure to file charges against her.

No, it was better to do the time. Nearly a week had passed already, and so far she'd survived reasonably intact. She touched her ass as she thought this, feeling the welted, abraded skin. Every day he whipped, cropped, flogged or spanked her, marking her in some fashion. Sometimes when he'd left her for the night, even though she knew he might be watching, she would stand in front of the mirror he kept near the cabinet, and crane back to see the damage he'd done that day.

She was both horrified and transfixed by the marks she saw—stripes of red and pink, some faded to white or flowered into little purple bruises. *I took that*, she found herself thinking with a curious kind of pride. *I endured that whipping, I handled that beating. I am strong. I can take whatever he gives me.*

Odder still was her physical reaction when she stared at the welts and bruises. Her pussy would moisten and swell and her nipples tingled with the remembered touch of his fingers and mouth. Perhaps because so often the pain of a punishment was mixed with the pleasure of sexual release. He would let her come, or force her to come, after or even during a beating. The sensations of stinging pain and burning pleasure had somehow fused in her brain, the memory of one eliciting the memory of the other in a tangle of fear and desire.

Sam sat down at his desk and swiveled his monitor toward her. "I was watching one of my favorite videos. It's giving me some nice ideas for you, slave girl." He pressed the play button. Rae stared at the screen. A tall, naked man with a shaved head stood in front of a young woman who was tied face down on a padded table. The man held the woman's head in his large hands as he guided his sizable cock into her mouth.

Rae stared, fascinated as the camera angle shifted, showing the woman from behind. The man had moved behind her and was pressing what looked like a large Plexiglas plug into the woman's ass. It was attached to a long silver hook with a rope hanging from it. The plug slipped inside, leaving only the shiny hook showing. The man walked around the tethered woman, rope in hand, until he again stood in front of her, his cock waving in her face, the rope pulled taut in his big fist, straining at the silver hook.

"Jesus," Rae whispered, before she realized she was speaking. She clamped her mouth shut and glanced nervously at Sam, aware she'd spoken out of turn. But Sam just smiled at her, an evil glint in his eye.

Rae watched as Sam lifted his hips and slid his shorts down his legs, kicking them aside. His cock sprang free, not quite fully erect, but definitely getting there. Rae felt a twinge in her pussy and her nipples perked, which confused her. She was supposed to hate this man. She told herself that a hundred times a day, but she couldn't deny he was a gorgeous specimen of male beauty, his cock straight and thick, his thighs muscular. She could see the blond hairs glinting in the light like spun gold on his tan skin.

He was pointing to the floor between his legs. "On your knees. I want you to suck my cock while I watch the rest of the movie." The video continued to play on the screen. The man was slapping the woman in the face, over and over, while she breathlessly begged him to do it again, and again! He still held the rope that was attached to the silver hook. Didn't that hurt? She was staying very still, but who wouldn't with that thing stuck up their ass?

Sam startled Rae by jerking her hair hard, forcing her to look away from the video. "Focus on my cock, not the screen. Don't stop until you make me come. And make sure you swallow every drop or I'll have you lick it up."

Swallowing nervously, Rae reached for Sam's cock, smelling his musky heat as she lowered her lips tentatively over the head. He was big, larger than she was used to, and she hoped she'd be able to satisfy him. She'd never had trouble pleasing a man in this way before, but she'd never been that man's personal sex slave either. She knew she'd better do a good job, or she'd definitely pay a price for it.

She reached for his balls, cupping them gently in one hand while she curled the fingers of her other hand around the base of his shaft. He spread his legs farther apart and shifted slightly in the chair, angling his hips forward.

She licked and sucked at the top half of his cock for a while, using her hands to provide stimulation lower down. "Take it farther," she heard him say from above. Rae could hear the woman on the video, her gasps and cries punctuated by the smacking sound of leather against skin. It was oddly discomfiting to realize Sam was focused not on her, but on the porn video on his monitor.

She felt almost incidental, just a tool to get him off, an object not that different from the vibrating wand he used on her. She told herself she should be glad. It was better *not* to be the focus of his sadistic intentions. *Just do what he wants and get it over with,* she told herself. *Then you can have a shower and breakfast.*

She moved her hand up the rigid shaft, meeting it with her lips over the fat crown of his cock. "Hands behind your back," she heard him say. "Take it all the way." She felt Sam's hand, heavy on the back of her head, pressing her forward onto his shaft.

Reluctantly, she took her hands away. He kept his hand on her head, his cock moving deeper into her mouth and past her soft palette, not stopping until the tip was lodged far back in her throat. He'd moved slowly enough so as not to gag her, but he held her there for several long seconds.

She couldn't get a breath, not the way his cock was blocking her windpipe. She tried to pull back but he held her fast. She felt a wave of panic rolling from her gut. She tried to empty her mind and relax her body.

He won't let you suffocate. You can trust him.

All at once she relaxed. What a startling thing to realize. She did trust him. She trusted Sam Ryker, the man who was holding her prisoner in his dungeon, the man who had basically raped her the first day, and done all sorts of horrible things to her ever since. She *trusted* him? Was she losing her mind?

She realized the pressure on the back of her head had eased and she slid back, sucking in oxygen as her lips glided along the smooth, warm skin of his cock. He groaned. "Yeah. That's it, babe. Show me what you can do." She lowered her head again, taking his full length, farther than she would have gone on her own, if he hadn't showed her just now that she could do it.

She moved back and forth, lifting herself slightly over him so she could take him deep into her throat again, and again, until he began to moan in a steady murmuring rhythm. "Yeah, yeah, oooooh, yeah, baby. Do it."

All at once she felt his fingers digging sharply into her shoulders as his body stiffened and arched forward. He thrust his shaft down her throat, nearly gagging her, but she managed to keep her muscles relaxed enough to receive him as he jerked against her. His fingers were gripping her hard, holding her fast as he ejaculated in several spasms.

The come shot past her tongue, sliding down her throat so that she didn't even need to swallow. He held himself that way for several moments, though he eased his grip on her shoulders. Finally he sagged back in his chair. Rae glanced up at him. Sam's eyes were closed, his lips parted. He had a blissful look on his face that almost made her smile. If he'd been her lover, not her jailer, she would have reached up and put her arms around his waist and kissed him.

Instead she leaned back on her heels and dared a glance at the screen. The couple was now dressed in identical black bathrobes, cuddling on a sofa while they discussed the scene they'd just enacted. Of course, it was just a scene, a show put on for the benefit of paying viewers.

"That was good," Sam announced from above her. "Stand up. I want to take your temperature."

Rae felt her face heating. She hated when he did that. He always pretended she was hot for him, even when she'd wanted to spit in his face. But she stood just the same, aware it would be worse for her if she disobeyed.

"Lean back against the desk," he instructed. "Brace yourself with your hands and spread your legs. Show me my cunt." He pushed a stack of papers from the cluttered desk and pointed to the cleared area. Reluctantly, Rae did as she was told. Though he regularly examined her pussy, she still hadn't gotten used to his scrutiny.

He licked his third finger and inserted it gently into her. He smiled that shit-eating grin of his. "Exactly as I thought. You're soaking wet, though whether it's from watching that guy on the video whip that girl, or from sucking my cock, it's hard to say."

The phone rang, making Rae jump. They both turned toward it, letting it ring a second and third time.

"I might as well get it," Sam said, his mouth curling into an evil smile. "Your job is to stay quiet, got it? You make a peep and you'll pay, I promise."

His finger still buried in her pussy, he reached with his other hand for the receiver. "Sam Ryker."

He listened a while and then began to speak in technical jargon about some piece of programming code as he casually fingered her. He stood, moving to stand beside her as he pressed his finger deeper, crooking it in such a way until he found that hot, sweet spot.

She bit her lower lip to keep from making a sound and squeezed her eyes shut. No one had ever touched her the way he did. No one had ever been able to wrest such powerful reactions from her, even when she did her best to resist. Stealing a glance at Sam's face, she tried to squirm away slightly without being too obvious, but a stern look from Sam stopped her.

He continued to work his terrible, wonderful magic until, despite her best intentions, a long, low moan slipped from between Rae's lips. She began to buck and shake, unable to control the climax he was pulling from her. What did she do? Did she pull away? Did she ask permission while he was on the phone, though he'd told her to stay quiet?

"Oh god," she whispered, "please...may I..."

"Hold on a moment, will you, Jack?"

Sam put his hand over the receiver and turned toward Rae, his hand still cupping her sex, his fingers still moving inside her. "You are a very naughty girl," he said, his eyes twinkling. "I told you to stay still and quiet, and here you are trembling and moaning. Jack might hear you! What should I tell him is going on?"

"Sam! Sir, I'm sorry! I can't help it, oh!"

He continued his relentless fingering as she gasped helplessly. It was too late. She couldn't stop the tide of this orgasm if her life depended on it. She opened her mouth, trying to form the words to ask for permission, but only managing a guttural grunt as she hurled headlong into a crashing wave of pure sensation.

She sat up slowly, Sam's papers scattered at her feet, her heart still thumping. She must have passed out for a second or two and it took her a moment to orient herself. Sam still had the phone to his ear, though he'd resumed his seat. "You too, buddy. Give me a call if it happens again."

He cradled the receiver and looked up at her, raising his eyebrows. "I'd say a punishment is in order, wouldn't you?"

Rae sighed. What could she say?

Chapter 9

Rae barely tasted the waffles with strawberries Sam fed her that morning after her grooming and shower. She was waiting nervously to find out what her punishment would entail. She'd come to learn the difference between punishments and training. The trainings could still be brutal and painful, but the focus was more on the sexual pleasure he would pull from her while also subjecting her to various painful distractions. She might be sexually teased or tortured during a punishment, but she was never allowed to come. The punishment was about the suffering.

While Rae sipped at her coffee, Sam left her on the bed and returned with a long thin rod of about eighteen inches with a brown suede handle at one end. He whipped it in the air and let it land against the bed near her leg with a thwack. Rae jumped, startled and frightened by the sound.

"This is a cane. Have you ever been caned, Rae?"

Stupid question. But a direct one, so she answered docilely, "No, Sir."

Sam ran his fingers over the smooth surface of the cane. "I should cane your cunt, since that's what you can't seem to control." Instinctively Rae crossed her legs and wrapped her arms around her torso. Sam went on, "But since you've never been caned, we'll start with your ass." He pointed to the floor. "Kneel beside the bed and lean over it, hands over your head on the mattress. I'll give you five good strokes on each side, and one on each breast for good measure. Then for training, we'll work on orgasm control, a skill in which you are sorely lacking."

Rae barely processed what he was saying, having homed in on the words, *five good strokes on each side...one on each breast.* Was he serious! She'd seen a horrible news story once about a man who'd been caned as punishment for his crime in Singapore. They'd showed pictures of his back after the caning — long, cruel stripes dripping with blood!

She felt herself growing dizzy and the food she'd just eaten sat like a stone in her belly. She looked up at Sam with pleading in her eyes. "I can't..." she whispered. "Blood..."

She had forgotten to ask for permission to speak. She tried to swallow but it felt like there were bits of glass in her throat. She blew out a shuddery breath. Sam sat on the bed beside her. Instead of yelling at her for speaking out of turn, he said, "Make no mistake, this will be a punishment you won't soon forget." He put his hand on her thigh, his voice gentler. "I'll mark you, but I won't break the skin. That's dangerous with a cane and could lead to infection and scarring."

Before Rae could even register her relief, he stood, suddenly unsheathing a sharp glance and turning it on her full force. He pointed to the ground. "Get into position. Now."

Rae scrambled off the bed and knelt. "That's it," Sam said. "Lean over on the mattress and lift your body up so your ass is on the edge of the bed, feet still on the ground." Rae did as instructed, her toes barely touching the carpet, her ass exposed for the cane. When she felt it moving over her skin, she flinched and jerked with fearful anticipation.

He began easily at first, lightly tapping the skin with the flat of the cane, creating a tingling in her flesh. She knew this was just warm up, and she remained tense with anticipation. "Breathe," he said from above her. "In and out, take it easy. You know it hurts worse if you clench your muscles. You can make it hard, or you can give in to what's going to happen anyway. You need to learn to flow with the pain, Rae. Stop fighting it at every turn."

Knowing he was right, Rae tried to do as he said, breathing in slowly and then exhaling just as slowly, in and out, in and out…

The first real blow whistled in the air, landing with a crack on her left cheek. Rae squealed and gripped the sheets tight in her fingers. "Good," Sam said. "Just a few days ago and you'd have been trying to cover yourself. You are making good progress, slave girl, in learning to accept the punishments you earn."

The second blow sliced across her other cheek, leaving a line of searing fire in its wake. "Fuck!" Rae screamed, the word wrenched from her without her being able to stop it.

The third blow caught both cheeks at once, low down where her thighs met her ass and Rae yelped, her nerve endings screaming. She felt sweat breaking out over her body and she was twisting the sheets in fingers cramping from her fierce grip. The cane rained fire down on her skin as she cried out, flinched and jerked but somehow managed to stay in position.

"Now for your breasts," Sam said, lightly tapping her shoulder with the tip of the cane. "Kneel up and offer them. Cup them in your hands and offer them for the cane."

Knowing she had no choice, Rae forced herself upright and off the bed. She turned and knelt in position, lightly resting her stinging ass cheeks against her heels. Her hands were trembling as she lifted her breasts. Squeezing her eyes shut, she turned her head away, biting her lip so hard she nearly drew blood.

"Rae. Face me. Open your eyes. You are to watch the cane. One on each breast. If you look away, I'll start over, do you understand?"

Rae forced herself to face Sam and she opened her eyes, though her lips remained compressed with fear. Sam moved to the side a little and lifted the cane. It came down on her right breast first and she watched in horrified fascination as a line appeared, first white and then turning rapidly to crimson red.

"Oh!" she gasped. Before she could react, the cane came down again, this time on her left breast, drawing a second line of white that morphed into red, the skin rising in a ridge of angry protest. Rae felt sweat breaking out on her upper lip. There was an unpleasant ringing in her ears, and her vision seemed to be narrowing into a tunnel of white. She dropped her breasts and let her head fall heavily forward.

All at once she felt Sam lifting her into his strong arms. Despite the fact he was the one who had done this to her, she found herself curling in against his chest, hiding her face in the dark blond curls at his sternum as he cradled her against him.

He sat on the bed, rocking Rae gently in his arms until the dizziness subsided, the horrible ringing receded and her vision cleared. She stayed still and quiet, enjoying the feel of his strong arms around her. There was blond stubble on his jaw that gave him a roguish look. He smelled good, like sandalwood and manly sweat. She had a sudden crazy impulse to lick his chest, to taste the salt on his skin. Instead she burrowed deeper into his arms, wishing she could just stay there forever.

But all too soon he loosened his grip and rolled her gently onto the bed beside him. He ran a finger along the welts on her breasts—two long ridges, red against the pale skin. Leaning over, he ran his tongue in a teasing circle around the areola and then suckled at the nipple, pulling it taut as it fattened in his mouth. He did the same with the other nipple. Rae couldn't deny it felt wonderful.

She moaned her approval, savoring the feel of his lips and tongue on her body. In a way, she realized with some surprise, his sensual touch felt even better juxtaposed against the lingering sting from the caning. Pleasure and pain...mingling, mixing, creating something strange and powerful that she didn't really understand but on some level she was coming to expect, to accept, to...need?

~*~

Luscious, lovely girl. Sam wanted nothing more than to drag his tongue down between her breasts, over the soft rise of her belly and down, down between her legs. He wanted to lap at her spicy-sweet wetness, to feel the swell of her desire and hear her breathy cries as he brought her to orgasm.

He could sense she was nearing a place, if not of acceptance, at least of acknowledgment on some level, that she needed what he offered. No, offered wasn't the correct term, and Sam was nothing if not a stickler for precision. He was forcing it on her — at least this setting, with its locks and chains and enforced behaviors had been forced upon her. True, she'd agreed to the terms, but only, in her mind, as the lesser of two evils.

Would there come a time when she craved the whip, longed for the cut of the cane, climaxed from having her pussy smacked while she was thoroughly trussed and bound? Or had he ruined any real chance of a love affair by claiming prematurely what he should have nurtured and coaxed into being?

Damn it, what was he even thinking? This wasn't anything approaching a love affair! It was blackmail, pure and simple. He had blackmailed her into submitting to his BDSM fantasies to avoid facing certain jail time on felony charges. Was he really any better than she was? If she was beginning to respond to the constant stimulation and forced arousal, it might easily be nothing more than a survival mechanism — seeking what little pleasure she could in a terrifying situation.

What the hell was he doing?

Punishing her. She stole a lot of money from me and my company. Not only that, anyone can see she's a born submissive, even if she denies it to herself.

Yes, he thought, willing himself to believe it because he wanted it so much to be true, *she wants this! She would never have had the courage or the honesty to seek it out herself, but I knew from that one time together, I knew — she was born for this. It's what she needs. It's where she belongs.*

Thus reassured for the moment, Sam stood. Rae rolled toward him, opening her eyes. Her lips were parted, her nipples shiny and hard from his kisses. It was a perfect time to introduce her to the nipple clamps. He would incorporate it into her orgasm control training. He stared down at her, feeling his power surging through his veins like a drug.

~ 140 ~

Eager to get started, he retrieved the clover clamps and fishing weights. Returning to the bed, he led Rae to stand beneath the large eyebolts he'd installed in the ceiling and rigged with hanging rope. Cuffs already dangled conveniently at the ends, waiting for feminine wrists. Sam brought a wooden stool over and set it beneath the hooks.

"Sit on the edge, knees spread, hips forward, cunt accessible," he ordered, for the moment ignoring his rising erection as Rae perched uncertainly on the edge of the stool, which was low enough to allow her to keep her feet flat on the ground. "Lift your arms so I can cuff you." Again she obeyed, watching with wide eyes as he secured her wrists in the cuffs and adjusted the ropes until her arms were raised over her head, which also lifted her lovely breasts for the attention they were about to receive.

Sam showed her the clamps. "These are called clover clamps," he explained, assuming she'd never seen a pair, BDSM virgin that she claimed to be. He pushed one end together to show how it opened and then let it close. "These go on your nipples. The cool thing about these clamps, versus the screw-on type, is they won't fall off if the chain between them is tugged." He smiled, his cock hardening at the fear in her eyes. "On the contrary, they just clamp tighter."

He reached for her right nipple. Rae tried to shrink back, but cuffed as she was, she wasn't going anywhere. Pulling the nipple taut, he let the clamp close over it.

He'd chosen his loosest pair but knew the pinch would still register.

Rae squealed and stared down at her ensnared nipple while Sam calmly subjected the second one to the same treatment.

"Please, sir, may I speak?" she gasped.

"Yes."

"It hurts! Ow, it hurts, please take them off. Please, please, please!"

Sam smiled, shaking his head. "You'll get used to it. In fact, after a while the compression creates a numbing effect. That's why I have these." He held up two lead teardrop-shaped weights with small clips attached at the tops. These he proceeded to attach to the chain between the clamps, drawing an anguished cry of "Ah!" from Rae's lips.

"Today's training," Sam said, pretending to ignore her suffering, "will be orgasm control. Your task is to focus on your cunt, not your nipples, *but*," he paused and then repeated for emphasis, "but you are *not* to come. Not until I say so. You are not to ask permission, you are not to tell me you can't help it. You are simply *not to come* until I say so." He took her chin between forefinger and thumb, forcing her face up as he looked down into her eyes. "Do I make myself crystal clear?"

"Yes, Sir," Rae whispered, her face still twisted with pain from the clamps. She would soon forget all about them—he'd make sure of that.

Sam retrieved the Hitachi stand, setting it up between Rae's legs. "Keep your legs open wide until I tell you otherwise. No matter what, you are not to close your legs to me." Obediently, Rae spread her legs wider, her sweet, bare pussy spread for him.

Sam squirted lubricant over the head of the vibrating wand and then rubbed the excess from his fingers along Rae's spread cleft. She drew in her breath but knew better than to close her legs. He positioned the stand until the head of the vibrator was at her cunt.

He flicked the switch and watched her.

The vibrations made the chain between her breasts sway, the heavy lead weights bumping together. Rae's eyes were closed, her brow furrowed, her teeth worrying her lower lip. Sam let the pressure build a while and then flicked the switch again, increasing the speed of its vibration.

Rae shuddered and grunted, leaning back and letting her wrists hold her weight. It wasn't long before he recognized the trembling in her limbs and the flush on her chest that signaled an impending orgasm. Her eyes flew open and she stared at him though, to her credit, she didn't speak.

But he knew what she was asking with her eyes. "No," he said. He lowered the speed on the vibrator and shifted it slightly, allowing her some recovery time. He lifted the weighted chain between her breasts and tugged lightly, drawing a ragged cry of pain from her lips as the tension tightened on her tortured nipples.

He dropped the chain and turned up the vibrator again, which whirred between her legs. "Oh, oh, oh!" she began to chant, as the vibrator relentlessly teased and tickled her clit.

"Hold it," Sam ordered. "Show some control. You *will not* come until I say so." He pulled the vibrator away, giving her a chance to catch her breath. Reaching for the lubricant bottle, he squeezed a little more over the head. Her cunt was red and swollen, the labia glistening.

He pushed the Hitachi back into place and Rae almost immediately began to shudder, her labia hypersensitized from the constant stimulation. Again and again he brought her just to the edge, ordering her to hold it, to control herself. She did remarkably well, lasting longer than he'd expected. But she would fail. By definition she would fail. There was only so long will power could win over the onslaught of the Hitachi's relentless vibrations.

Damp tendrils of hair curled along her flushed cheeks and rivulets of sweat rolled down her sides and between her breasts. A low, feral moan rose in her throat and erupted in a keening cry as she climaxed, her body wracked with shuddering spasms.

Sam pulled the Hitachi stand away and crouched in front of Rae as her shuddering eventually subsided. She sagged hard against her cuffs, her head lolling forward. Gently, Sam lifted her chin and pushed the damp hair out of her face.

"Dear, dear, dear," he said with mock dismay. He shook his head, though he couldn't quite hide the small smile pushing its way onto his lips. "You came before I said you could. I guess we'll just have to keep working on this particular exercise until we get it right."

He watched the play of emotions move over Rae's face like a storm. She wanted to protest, to say it wasn't fair — that she couldn't help it, that he'd tricked her, but then, as quickly as it had washed over her features, it was gone. She gazed at him impassively, almost serenely.

Sam nodded his silent approval, but there was no getting around what must come next. "You do know, slave girl, what happens when you disobey?"

"Yes, Sir," she whispered.

"Tell me."

"I get punished."

"That's correct. And this — " Sam released the clamps without warning, pulling them roughly from her tortured nipples. As the blood raced back, reawakening the compressed nerve endings with a vengeance, Rae screamed with pain. " — is your punishment."

Chapter 10

Rae opened the drawer of the nightstand and felt inside for the little balls of tissue, counting them with her fingers. After the fourth day holed up in Sam's dungeon, she'd decided to keep track of her incarceration and had come up with this method. She had managed to secret a few squares of toilet paper in her hand that day after her shower. She had hid it beneath her pillow and now, each morning when she woke up she tore off a tiny piece, rolled it into a ball and slipped it into the drawer. If Sam had observed her doing this, he hadn't said anything about it.

Turning onto her back, Rae stretched her legs, which were a little stiff from yesterday's cycling. Sam had decided a week into her captivity that Rae needed to exercise each day. He'd brought in an old stationary exercise bike he kept in a storage room just off the dungeon, along with a yoga mat. He had her cycle and stretch every day for at least thirty minutes. Though she wished he didn't have to watch her, she was grateful for the chance to use her muscles.

One, two, three…Rae pushed each little ball in the otherwise empty drawer aside as she counted. There were fourteen balls. She dropped in the fifteenth and pushed the drawer closed. Halfway done with her sentence.

Halfway to...to what really?

She would have no job with *Ryker Solutions* when he let her out—that was understood. Sam would never let Rae work for him again, nor would she want to. She could go back to commercial banking, she thought with a shudder, but knew she wouldn't. She had enjoyed the freedom of working as a freelance financial consultant too much to go back to some cubicle and clock in nine to five.

She would have to move. Manhattan was too expensive anyway and besides, it would always remind her of Sam. She'd move somewhere she could afford, set out her shingle and get to work earning enough to both support herself and to pay Sam back. Even if she never saw him again, she'd promised herself he'd get back every penny she'd borrowed.

Okay, every penny she'd *stolen*.

Then, somehow, she'd face the rest of her life.

Rae had taken to waking several minutes before Sam did his wakeup call through the monitor. The room was softly illuminated by two nightlights plugged in along the walls. While waiting, she would stare at the ceiling, letting thoughts drift idly through her mind.

I wonder if we'll have scrambled eggs this morning. I hope there's orange juice. I wish the chain was a little longer so I could scratch my ankle without contorting. I hope I get to come today. I wonder what it will be like when I see sunshine and grass again. I miss wearing clothes. I wonder if I'll get to suck his cock today.

She would think back over the latest training or punishment, pondering how she could have done better, or what had pleased Sam or, though she was getting much better at avoiding this, what had angered him.

Intellectually she knew she should hold on to the rage that had peppered and shaped her first week, but it took too much energy. And what was the point? When she was a good girl, Sam rewarded her with delicious food and other nice things. He let her come almost every day, though admittedly she earned it in one way or another.

She had learned to work through the pain to get to the pleasure awaiting her. Sometimes they were all mixed up—just as she felt the delicious release of a powerful orgasm, it would be tempered by the sting of a whip or the hard smack of a wooden paddle that would leave bruises on her ass for several days. Her body understood even when her mind rejected the notion, that in order for her to take her pleasure, she had to also endure the pain.

As the days edged into weeks, she no longer questioned this. She accepted it. Lately though it had gone beyond acceptance. Though she was scarcely able to admit it to herself, she *wanted* the pain. No, that wasn't right. She didn't want it! That was sick! And yet... And yet, somehow, she needed it in order to give power and meaning to the pleasure.

How could that be correct? Did she really crave the cut of the single tail? Did she revel in the viselike pressure of the clamps painfully compressing her nipples or tugging at her labia? Did she want to be tied down and subjected to Sam's bizarre humiliations, just so she could come at his command?

It was too complicated and unsettling to think about. Better to focus on what she could control. Such as how many times he'd let her come today. With his permission, of course.

She'd learned her lesson on day nine. She certainly didn't want a repeat of that day! At the time she'd been furious because she felt like he'd tricked her by yet again forcing her into coming with that damn vibrating wand, even while he was commanding her not to.

Truth be told, she probably could have held out longer — he'd been training her in what he called orgasm control — but she'd been tired and very aroused by the extended nipple play from earlier that morning. She'd earned that orgasm, damn it, or so she had told herself when she let go and rode the sweet climax to its shuddering conclusion.

Afterwards, she was punished with orgasm denial. Worse, he'd left her alone for such a long time. She'd found, to her confusion, that she missed him. Even being tied up and tortured was better than being left alone. But after the stolen orgasm, he'd chained her to the bed and left her there.

It had felt more like a week than a day, the hours trickling by like thick sap dripping down a tree trunk, and just about as exciting. With nothing else to distract her, she'd focused on the cunt she wasn't allowed to touch, her mind racing with images of Sam, naked with his hard cock in his hand, guiding it to her mouth, or Sam, his eyes blazing as he cuffed her to the St. Andrew's Cross for an extended flogging session that invariably ended with a mind-numbing orgasm as he finger-fucked her until she begged for release.

After being not only permitted, but ordered to come sometimes as often as ten or fifteen times over a twenty-four hour period, and then being denied for so many hours—it had been like withdrawing from a particularly addictive drug.

He had stripped away the bedding so she couldn't do anything sneaky. He'd said he'd be watching and if he saw her hands get anywhere near her cunt, he'd deny her for *another* twenty-four hours. She drifted in and out of restless, agitated sleep during the enforced captivity on her bed, her nipples aching for attention, her cunt swollen and wet with need.

Yes, she'd learned her lesson, all right. Since then she never came without permission and she never touched her body (*his* body, he would remind her) when she was alone.

"Good morning, slave girl." Sam's rich, deep voice shook Rae at once from her reverie.

"Good morning, Sir," she said to the empty room as she tumbled from the bed to the floor, lifting the long chain that extended from her collar to the headboard with practiced ease so it wouldn't tangle. She knelt up, placing her hands behind her neck and spreading her knees wide.

Maybe he'll have strawberries for me this morning. I like when he pops them into my mouth, one by one, his eyes never leaving mine...

After grooming and breakfast (no strawberries, but chocolate croissants, even better) Sam brought a large duffel bag from the cabinet and took it to the eyebolts embedded in the ceiling. The eyebolts usually meant suspension and intense whipping or flogging sessions. Rae's ass was still sore and marked from yesterday's caning. Was he planning to mark her again so soon?

Sam was wearing white shorts, his torso bare. Rae had come to learn when he wore those shorts it usually meant she would be sucking his cock before the hour was up. This suited Rae, who had come to crave his musky sweetness, savoring the salty gush of his ejaculate on her tongue and even more, the look of intense pleasure and vulnerability washing over his face at the moment of orgasm. Afterwards he would sometimes pull her into his arms, if only for a moment.

Rae felt her cunt tingling with anticipation, deeply curious as to what was in the duffel bag. Without speaking or looking at her, Sam pulled out four thick lengths of chain and attached them to the four outermost bolts, creating a square between the four chains. Next he extracted a large rectangle of black leather with long straps at each corner, a large O ring sewn into the end of each strap. He clipped the rings to the chains, creating a kind of hammock.

Turning at last to her, he said, "I'm pleased with your progress over the past several days and I've decided to reward you with my cock." As he spoke, Sam massaged his erection, clearly visible beneath the thin fabric of his shorts. His words of praise warmed her, causing a rush of grateful heat to move into her cheeks.

But what did he mean exactly? She looked at the leather hammock, trying to imagine how he was going to have her suck his cock. Would he be in the hammock? Was she to stand over him? How would it work? She voiced none of this. A slave did not speak out of turn.

Sam reached for her hand and pulled her upright, lifting her effortlessly into his arms. He deposited *her* into the hammock, which now completely confused her, but still she asked nothing. She knew he would tell her what to do. She waited, swaying gently in the makeshift swing, for his instruction.

He produced four Velcro cuffs. "Scoot your ass to the edge of the sling." She obeyed, holding on to the chains behind her to keep from falling. He attached a cuff to each wrist, securing her arms in place against the chains.

"Now your legs. Lift them as high as you can along the front chains."

Feeling awkward but determined to obey, Rae did as she was told. Sam cuffed her ankles in place, so her weight was resting on her ass, her cunt splayed wide on the edge of the sling. The back of the sling supported her back and neck but didn't stop her from feeling extremely vulnerable in this exposed position.

She watched as he pulled his shorts down and kicked them away, revealing his erect cock, bobbing from the thatch of dark blond pubic curls at his groin.

He spit onto his hand and fisted his cock, stepping closer to stand between her spread legs. "Oh!" she said involuntarily, suddenly understanding what he'd meant by his earlier comment. *I've decided to reward you with my cock.*

He was going to fuck her!

Not since that one time early on had he penetrated her with his cock. He'd used dildos and plugs, as well as his fingers and even once, his tongue, but never again had he fucked her. She'd told herself she was glad — and at first she had meant it. At first she'd thought of what he'd done as a rape, and nursed her rage and outrage, telling herself she was relieved he hadn't tried anything like that again.

But lately, well, for quite a while actually, if she was honest, she'd been fantasizing about what it would feel like to be filled again with that thick, long cock. Sometimes in the night she would wake from a sensual dream, her body aching to feel his girth stretching her, stroking her, claiming her...

Now it was happening. This was no dream.

Without speaking he moved closer, guiding his shaft into her opening. He moved carefully, not like the plunging thrust from behind when she'd been tethered to the sawhorse. Instead, almost gently, he guided his full length into her. Gripping her ankles, he pulled her forward, which caused his cock to penetrate even deeper. The head of his cock touched something inside her that caused a tremor of white hot pleasure to hurtle through Rae's body. She gasped from the unfamiliar but intense sensation.

He began to push the sling away and then draw it forward, nearly withdrawing from her and then thrusting deep, deeper than she'd ever been penetrated, touching that sweet spot again and again. Something about the angle of the sling and the way she was suspended worked together to create an incredible sensation inside her—like a thousand fingers moving and twisting, touching every sensitive nerve and fiber in ways they'd never been touched before.

In and out he moved, using the swing's momentum to pull her onto and then off of his cock. Rae gripped the chains tight and let her head fall back, giving herself over to the eddying currents of pure pleasure coursing through her body. Dimly, she was aware she would have to pay later—pleasure in Sam's dungeon never came without a price—but for now she didn't care. She was in heaven, his cock pulsing inside her as she moaned and trembled.

She held on as long as she could, not sure if she was going to be allowed to come, praying that he didn't forbid what soon she wouldn't be able to resist. "Oh god!" she finally cried. "Please, Sir, may I? Can I? Oh god, please..."

"Do it. Come for me." Sam leaned over her, buried to the hilt, his balls slapping at her ass. His hands were on her breasts, sure fingers rolling and twisting her distended nipples, adding that edge of pain she found she now needed to fully surrender.

His face was nearly touching hers, his lips inches from her own. Without quite realizing what she was doing, Rae turned her face so their lips touched. She let hers part and snaked her tongue along his bottom lip.

All at once his mouth was on hers, his tongue moving against hers in time to the cock thrusting hard in her sex. She gave herself over to it all, the cock, the orgasm, his kiss, his perfect, consuming kiss...

~*~

Her eyes were closed, her lips curved in a satisfied, post-orgasmic smile. Sam's cock was still hard inside her, his balls tight. She might be done, but he wasn't.

He pulled his cock from her slippery wetness. She stirred but didn't open her eyes. Cuffed as she was to the four chains that supported the sling, with her ass perched on the edge, she was completely exposed, not only her cunt, but the tiny pink bud of her asshole.

Sam realized the height and position of the sling were perfect for anal sex. Had she ever done it before?

To test her reaction, he guided the head of his cock until it was touching her nether hole. He pushed gently against the tight ring of muscle guarding the entrance.

Rae's eyes flew open. "What?" she began anxiously. She was gripping the chains above her cuffed wrists and he could see the fear in her eyes. So she was an anal virgin. The thought excited him. He would be the first to claim her ass, to show her how to submit in yet another way to him.

"Is this your first time?"

"Yes. No! I mean, I don't allow—that is…" Cutting herself off, she bit her lower lip, no doubt aware she was about to tread on dangerous ground. Sam nodded approvingly at her newfound ability to control her tongue. That was good. She was coming to realize she didn't have that kind of say any longer, not while she was in his dungeon.

She tried again. "Sam…Sir, please, I don't, I can't—"

"Take it easy, Rae. I'm not going to hurt you. But I want to fuck your ass. It's another way you can give yourself to me, and it's what I want." Gripping her shoulders to hold the sling still, he nudged at the tight bud with his cock. Rae whimpered and gasped. He could feel the rigid tension in her muscles and he stepped back, taking stock of his slave girl.

"You need to calm down. Remember to focus on the relaxation techniques I've taught you. Slow your breathing. Deep, slow breaths. Relax your body and open yourself to me. Your tension shows me you aren't in a submissive state of mind. You aren't where I want you to be. Where you need to be."

Her wide, blue eyes fixed on his face, Rae actually made an effort to do as he said. She drew in a deep, shuddery breath and expelled it slowly through pursed lips.

"That's it." Sam smiled encouragingly. "Anal sex doesn't have to hurt, you know. It can be a very pleasurable experience."

He left her long enough to retrieve a tube of lubricant. He squirted a dollop onto his fingers and lightly probed between her ass cheeks. Carefully he pushed his finger into the tight opening, moving in small circles inside her as he pressed deeper. At first her muscles clamped down hard, but Sam took his time, moving slowly and gently, all the while watching her face, gauging her reaction.

When he felt the muscles ease, he added a second finger, widening the circle of muscle, his cock throbbing impatiently for its turn. Rae was breathing slower, though her eyes remained fixed on his, the fear in them still sharp.

Sam guided the head of his cock again between her spread cheeks. This time it slipped in easily. He felt the grip of muscle massage his cock, its hold tighter than a cunt but less yielding.

Rae gasped and yelped. Sam scanned her face, noting the fear but also the excitement in her eyes. His cock hardened to steel inside her. Using her hips to pull her forward, he pushed himself all the way in, slipping past rings of muscle, letting her body adjust to his girth. Rae yelped again, her breath coming in rapid pants. Her knuckles were white, her fingers gripping the chains like lifelines.

"Hey, calm down," Sam soothed, trying to keep his raging lust in check at least a while longer. His cock ached with the need to thrust itself inside her, to pummel her until she begged for mercy. He wanted to ram into her, to feel the tight clamp of her muscles massaging him to a powerful orgasm.

But he forced himself to go slow, not wanting to tear the delicate muscle and membrane. Rae's body was still taut with anxiety, all the easy languor of her climax gone. Sam's mind told him this was fine — she was his slave, not his lover and should take what he gave her, no matter how she felt about it. But his heart said otherwise. He realized, as dangerous as the admission was, that he wanted her to enjoy the experience. He wanted to make her first time something she remembered not with fear, but with pleasure.

Remaining buried deep inside her, he pressed his thumb against her hooded clit. With a feather-light touch, he moved the pad of his thumb in a circle, feeling her sweet spot swell at his touch. He continued to tease and arouse her until he felt her body relax a little. He noted with satisfaction that her fingers had loosened their death grip on the chains of the sling.

He began to move again inside her, using one hand to guide the sling so she was pulled back and forth onto his cock, the thumb of his other hand swirling over her slippery, swollen labia. Her anal passage held him in a tight, steady clutch as he moved inside her, punctuated by sudden muscle spasms that gripped him in a silky vise.

It wasn't long before he lost his resolve to draw out the experience. He could feel the shuddering rise of a climax being milked from his cock by her impossibly tight ass. When it came, it was almost a surprise, overtaking his senses, making him forget for that one moment to be cautious with his virgin slave.

He rammed hard into her as he released his seed, his groan of pleasure at odds with her sudden scream of pain. He pulled her closer, dropping his face to hers, muffling her cries with his kisses. As he kissed her mouth, his cock still buried inside her, he reached for the cuffs that kept her wrists tethered to the chains. He jerked them free, wanting her to put her arms around his neck, suddenly longing for her to pull him into a lover's embrace.

But her hands remained as they were, fingers curled tight around the chains. She turned her face from his kiss and pressed her lips together, keeping her eyes tightly closed.

Sam stood abruptly, stepping back and allowing his cock to pull from her body. She remained still, face averted, her legs lewdly spread. Moving quickly, Sam released the ankle cuffs and lifted Rae into his arms. As he carried her toward the bathroom for a shower, the foolish lover's fantasy of a moment before dissipated like a ribbon of smoke curling over her shoulder.

Chapter 11

Sam sat at his keyboard, staring at the same few lines of code he'd been wrestling with for the past two hours. He saved the work and turned away, getting up from his desk and going to stare out the window at his front lawn.

Two children went running by on the sidewalk, their mother following a moment later, pushing a baby stroller. "Slow down, boys!" he could hear her shout. "Don't cross the street till I get there!"

As the woman passed his house she turned her head, looking up suddenly, directly at Sam, as if she were scrutinizing his face; consigning it to memory. Instinctively he stepped back from the window, discomfited by the encounter.

Had she really been looking at him? Sam doubted it, yet nonetheless, her penetrating gaze had left him feeling...exposed.

He sat heavily on the sofa beneath the window and dropped his head into his hands. What was he doing? How could he continue to justify what was going on in his basement?

At first he'd been surprised but pleased at how easily she'd fallen into line. After those first few rough days when she still hadn't reconciled herself to her fate, she'd begun to obey him, if not exactly eagerly, at least without resisting at every turn.

He'd been working on aligning the pleasure and the pain in her psyche, teaching her to expect the one with the other, even to require it. As he'd suspected, she was a born submissive with strong masochistic tendencies. She was blossoming under his tutelage, each day more compliant and obedient than the next.

What had begun as punishment for her thievery had turned into more. Not only for her, but for himself. Yet he knew when the thirty days were up, she'd demand that he follow through on the terms they'd agreed upon.

More than once, especially when they were in the middle of an intense scene, with Rae naked and bound before him, submitting to his latest round of erotic torture, he'd found himself thinking he might never let her go.

Young women in New York City disappeared all the time. She'd once mentioned some family out in Nebraska, but he didn't think they were at all close. She had no roommate, and when her fictional month in Japan was at an end, who was there to know that she hadn't returned to her daily life?

Her landlord would keep her deposit, dispose of her things and easily re-rent the coveted apartment space. Sam had the key. Maybe he'd even go over there and clear it out. He could keep her stuff in the attic or just give it to charity.

When his mind veered in this bizarre direction, Sam had to pull himself up short. He wasn't some kind of monster, keeping a woman captive as his permanent slave girl, locked and naked in his dungeon, forever at his mercy...

Yet, wasn't he? Wasn't that precisely what he was doing? True, the captivity was finite. Only two weeks left until he had to give her up, but did that make what he was doing any less heinous?

Though it was only three in the afternoon, Sam went out into the kitchen and opened the liquor cabinet. He poured himself some vodka and added a few cubes ice. He drank the first one quickly, draining the glass before pouring a second one, which he took back into the study. He sat in front of the closed-circuit TV and gazed at the screen.

What was really bothering him, he knew, was what had happened earlier that day. Why had he decided to fuck her? He'd promised himself he wouldn't do that again, not after that first time. It was a boundary, albeit an artificial one, that gave him a sense of safety. As long as he didn't fuck her, they weren't lovers. He was just her part-time Master, her temporary Sir, her jailer. He was teaching her a lesson, exacting a penance, taking his due for her crime against him.

But she'd been so good lately. So obedient, so responsive, so in tune with his commands and dictates that he'd found himself falling...

No. No, he would not even go there.

Rae Johansen was a liar and thief. She was hot, yes, there was no denying that. And she was submissive, but he was not the Master for her. Their relationship, whatever it was, was forever sullied by her breach of his trust.

And by his exacting such a cost for that breach.

He stared at the screen. She was on her bed, as always. Indeed, he'd chained her there, telling her to rest while he did a little work. He would have her exercise in a while.

When he'd released her cuffs and helped her from the sling, she'd stared at him with those dark blue eyes flecked with bronze, her lips like crushed rose petals. There was more in her expression than obedience or even sexual satisfaction. If he hadn't known better he'd have thought there was...love?

No, impossible. He was fantasizing. She was his prisoner, his slave. No more, no less.

What had possessed him to kiss her? It was bad enough he'd succumbed to his weakness, desperate to be inside her, but the kiss? The intimacy of it had nearly left him undone. You could pay a hooker to let you fuck her, but not to kiss her.

Kisses were for lovers.

Rae Johansen was *not* his lover.

She was not even his friend. He'd sealed their fate with his strange choice of revenge. There could be no going back, or forward.

Sam tipped the last of the vodka into his mouth and stood, smashing his other fist into his thigh.

Damn it! Enough with the angst and the self-recrimination. She was getting off easy — thirty days instead of years in prison and a record that would follow her for life. Thirty days of letting him pretend to own her. Thirty days of dirty games. For that's all they were, in the end. Just games.

She was a quick study. He had to give her that. She was docile and obedient, compliant to his every demand. She even seemed to like what he gave her. She begged so sweetly to be allowed to come. She gasped so prettily when leather, wood and rattan struck her skin, leaving their fiery marks and making her cry...

They had two weeks left. Any lingering fantasy of Rae becoming his lover had long since been smashed by the reality of what he'd taken from her. The damage was already done, so why not enjoy what was left and finish the deed? She'd become a willing, even an eager, pupil, a good little submissive who waited each morning with her chin proudly up, her eyes cast down in respect.

She'd taken everything he'd given her. And yet there was always something held back. Something she kept private and on reserve. She hadn't yet truly submitted to him. She hadn't given him everything she had. Could he wrest that from her in the short time remaining? Did he dare?

What would it take to reach her—to truly reach the core of her submission?

Could he come up with something that would break through the façade of docility and obedience to find the real submissive woman beneath? Something that would challenge her? Something that would find and connect with her deepest-seated fear and longing? Something that would slip past the barriers and break her down?

Then he remembered.

That first time he'd groomed her—her near-panic at the thought of his using a razor on her, the way she still trembled, even now, when he shaved her. She would close her eyes, her lips compressed, her hands clenched into fists when he ran the sharp edge of the razor's blades over her skin. Her fear still radiated like heat, even after all this time.

Sam strode to his desk and slid open the top left drawer, extracting the black-handled pen knife he kept there. He flicked opened the silver blade and ran the edge of it lightly over the pad of his thumb.

"My slave girl," he said aloud, "is terrified at the sight of her own blood."

~*~

"What are you?"
"Your slave, Sir."
"What else?"

"Your submissive. Your cunt. Your property." Rae was standing at attention on the sixteenth night, her arms behind her back, hands grasping opposite elbows.

"While you are here, what will you do for me, for your Master?"

"Anything, Sir. Everything."

He had taught her to say these words and she obediently mouthed them, telling herself they meant nothing. Again and again he had drilled her on her responses and she'd learned to parrot them almost without thinking. They were just words, after all. They were just part of the game, a requirement of her enforced stay, nothing to do with her.

Stick and stones...

And yet somehow they slipped more easily off her tongue now, and along with the words came a curious kind of safety, of peace. She *belonged* to someone. Someone who took her in hand, removing all need for difficult decisions. He made her come like she never had in her life. Forget about faking orgasms—Sam pulled them from her, again and again until she was completely spent. He made her cry with both passion and pain but he was always there afterwards to hold her and soothe away the tears. He fed her, he bathed her, he kept her cocooned in the safety of carefully prescribed punishments and rewards.

Where had the formidable Ms. Rae Johansen, equal to any man in the bedroom or the boardroom, disappeared to? Or, and this thought shocked her the first time it had slipped mutinously into her mind, was that put-together professional woman the façade? Was that the posture she'd adopted to hide from secret submissive impulses she'd never before understood?

Probably she was only adapting—engaging in some sort of self-preservation to keep from going insane. Once she got the hell out of this bizarre prison, she'd resume her persona of strong, confident woman, subservient to no man.

And yet, there was no denying that when she was being whipped or sexually tortured, the constant whirring rush of her mind finally slowed and eased. She was able to focus fully and completely on what was happening to her. Whether this was a good or a bad thing, she wasn't entirely sure.

Sam was wearing his black leather pants and a white linen shirt, opened to reveal the blond curls on his powerful chest. Pretending she was gazing respectfully at the floor, she let her eyes glide over his lower half. There was something oblong and hard in his right hip pocket, but she forgot about it as she focused on the sexy bulge between his legs encased in the soft black leather.

The leather pants usually meant an intense BDSM session with very little sweetness involved. Oddly, instead of frightening her, this realization caused a tug of desire deep in Rae's cunt. Was she actually coming not only to endure, but to crave the pain?

He left Rae, heading toward the cabinet where he kept what he called his toys. He returned with something she recognized and held it out to her. "Put this on." He'd used this on her before and she knew what to do.

Rae took what looked like a string bikini made of thin leather straps. Where the crotch should be, instead there was a butterfly-shaped vibrator that fit between her legs, its center resting neatly on her clit. Sam held up the remote and turned it on the lowest speed, creating a pleasant, tickling hum at Rae's sex. The remote was clipped to a leather string, which Sam slipped over his left wrist, wearing it like a bracelet.

He led Rae to the chains that hung from the ceiling and cuffed her wrists so that her arms were suspended, but not pulled taut, still bent at the elbows. There were two black cotton sashes tied to the chains from the last time he'd suspended her there. He'd used them as gag and blindfold, but this time they were left hanging, which suited Rae, as being gagged and blindfolded had left her feeling vulnerable and nervous about what might come next.

Sam turned the remote a notch higher and Rae shifted slightly, enjoying the sensation of the butterfly, hoping he planned to let her come without too much suffering beforehand.

Sam reached into his pocket and withdrew the object she'd noticed earlier. He held it in front of Rae, slowly opening it. Rae stared, her heart leaping into her throat when she realized what it was.

"You're afraid of knives, aren't you, Rae? Of knives, needles, blood…" Rae fixated on the sharp blade and held her breath. Surely he wouldn't…he couldn't…

He touched the point of the blade to her right breast. Rae screamed and jerked back in her chains.

Sam lowered the knife, holding it at his side. "Direct question, slave."

"Yes," she whispered, her voice having retreated somewhere behind her fear. This wasn't part of the bargain. He had said he wouldn't harm her. Oh god, was he going to *kill* her?

Reading her mind, he shook his head, reaching with his free hand to stroke her cheek. "Calm down, Rae. I'm not going to harm you, silly girl. You are my prized possession."

He continued to stroke her, drawing his finger down her throat and along her breast. Despite her fear, her body reacted to his touch, her nipples perking, her clit throbbing against the soft rubber butterfly.

Sam was staring at her with a wild spark in his eyes—part passion, part power, part…love?

She had to believe him—he wouldn't harm her. Deep inside she knew she was ultimately safe with Sam. So, what then? Was this another test? There was no way in hell she would pass it.

"You speak the words I've taught you well enough and for the most part you take what I give you, but you continue to hold back the essence of your submission. I want to reach past the walls that keep us from truly connecting. I want to break them down. I want to tap into the pure masochist I think is waiting to be released inside you. It's not only something I want. It's something you need. It's something you've earned."

"No, Sam. Not the knife. I can't..." she pleaded, her voice breaking. She had spoken out of turn, but she couldn't help it. *Not the knife, not the knife, not the knife.*

He put his fingers to her lips. "Shh. You need to move through the fear. It's the only way to get to the other side of your true nature."

Rae shook her head, her eyes fixated on the bright silver blade as Sam lifted it again. This couldn't be happening. He wouldn't do this to her. She trusted him. He wouldn't hurt her. *Not the knife, not the knife, not the knife.*

"Here are the rules. I'm going to draw this blade over your skin. Your job is to stay very still. You wouldn't want me to accidentally cut you." He pressed the flat edge of the blade against her left breast. It was cold and hard and Rae shuddered at the touch.

Her heart was beating so loud she wondered if Sam could hear it. He moved the cold metal over her sternum, sliding it across her other breast. "Slow your breathing," he soothed. "You can do this. You will do it. For me. For us..."

Rae was trembling, and not only with fear, she realized, but with a sudden burst of pure rage. The anger she had put aside as she reconciled herself to her situation burst back into her consciousness like a runaway train. Over these past weeks she'd allowed herself to be lulled into some sort of dark dream. To think she'd almost believed herself safe, taken care of, protected, even loved! What a fool she had been. He would never stop. Nothing would satisfy his sadistic need to punish her, his quest to break her down, to terrorize her into submission.

"There is no *us*," she hissed, her voice dripping with fury.

The words slipped out before Rae even realized she was going to speak. She bit her lip, the rage subsiding back into pure fear as she stared at the pointed blade. She dragged her eyes away from it to gauge Sam's reaction to her outburst.

His face was a study of hurt and anger, his eyes flashing, his lips bunching, his nostrils flaring. As she stared, something overcame his features, like a shade sliding down over a window. The emotion drained away, leaving only a hard glint in his eye.

"Of course, you're right. There is no us." His voice was quiet and controlled, hard as steel. He lifted the knife and touched its point to the hollow of her throat, just below her slave collar.

~*~

There is no us.

The words reverberated in Sam's brain like a ricocheting bullet. He was startled at how much they hurt. Had he really fooled himself into thinking what they shared had anything to do with D/s or, even more ridiculously, with love?

Her hatred had shone like a bright flame when she spit out those words.

There is no us.

All at once he understood—her apparently growing submission was only her having learned over the days and weeks to better play the game. The same way she'd fooled him in business, pretending to be his ally and supporter, she had been fooling him now with a pretense of true submission.

What did you expect, Ryker? You've held her against her will in your fucking basement, keeping her naked and marked. Did you think she'd fall in love, you asshole? Was this ever about anything more than power and revenge?

Sam withdrew the knife from Rae's throat, leaving a small red dot behind on her skin. He stared at the knife in his hand, aware he should put it away. He was hurt, and letting that hurt manifest itself as anger. A Dom should never act out of anger with his sub. That was ingrained in his psyche, or it should have been.

But he wasn't her Dom, was he? And she certainly was no sub! He was an idiot to have assigned anything even remotely romantic to her reactions. She'd been acting a part, that was all. She was nothing more than a prisoner who had voluntarily consented to serve her time under his control, at his mercy.

Fine.

Let the prisoner suffer her just desserts.

Sam turned the butterfly remote to high, making it hum between Rae's legs. She drew in a sharp breath at the sudden intensity but there was no way she could escape the forced stimulation.

"Stay still," he reminded her. He lifted the knife again and dragged the point along her right forearm, scratching a thin pink line along her pale skin. She was watching, the fear bright in her eyes. He drew a second line on her other arm.

Carefully he pulled the point of the blade along the tops of her breasts. Rae was whimpering softly, her body trembling, though whether from the vibrator or the knife, Sam couldn't be sure.

He drew the blade down her left side and then her right, pressing slightly harder. Her skin was very sensitive to the knife, reddening quickly as it scraped her. Seized with a sudden idea, Sam began to trace a word on her stomach, just above her shaven mons.

C-U-N-T.

The word appeared in dark pink. She jerked in a sudden spasm just as he was finishing the T and the point slipped. She yelped but continued to convulse and he realized she was orgasming. She hadn't asked permission, naughty girl.

He nearly said something about her breach of protocol, but was distracted by the droplet of blood that appeared on her skin, an impossibly bright, holly red. He reached for the butterfly remote and turned it down to its lowest setting, allowing Rae to ease slowly off the orgasm.

The drop of blood rolled down, leaving a red path on her mons. Rae started to look down, but Sam stopped her with a hand to her throat. "Eyes straight ahead," he ordered, "or I'll blindfold you."

He realized his cock was hard, constrained in the leather and his heart was beating fast. He reached for his fly and pulled out his cock, giving it a few firm strokes. The sight of her blood had released something wild inside him—something powerful and edgy, something he had to explore.

He lifted the knife again and drew its point down her right thigh and then up her left one. He forced her legs farther apart and ran the blade along her inner thigh. "No!" she screamed, jerking away. Again the point slipped at her sudden movement and another droplet of the bright red blood appeared. Sam touched it, painting her soft skin with it, fascinated.

Lust fused with a kind of crazy energy was pulsing at his temples as he stared at the tethered beauty before him. The word *cunt* was still clearly visible, etched onto her fair skin. She was a cunt—his cunt. She deserved everything he gave her and more. He brought the blade to her skin again, drawing it upward. He slid it along her hip and slipped the point beneath the leather strap holding the vibrator in place. He yanked forward, cutting through the strap.

He did the same thing on the other side, and the butterfly fell to the carpet between Rae's feet. Sam turned it off and slipped the remote from his wrist, letting it fall as he kicked the vibrator away.

The prick on Rae's inner thigh continued to bleed, the blood rolling down her leg in a shiny red path. This time Sam's blade was deliberate as he crouched down and lightly nicked her other inner thigh, needing to see symmetry in a second line of blood.

He was aware Rae was crying, soft whimpering cries, but he could barely hear her over the pounding of his heart, thumping in his ears like a primitive drum. Standing, he stood face to face with his captive. Tears were rolling down her cheeks.

"Please," she begged. "Please stop. Please…"

He knew he should. There was something wild and dangerous coursing through him. He wasn't in control. It was as if some demon had taken over his better nature. His cock throbbed and twitched. He didn't want to hear her cries or see her frightened eyes. But he didn't want to stop either. It was no longer about her or her submission or her walls or any other poetic bullshit he'd made up to justify his own sadistic actions.

It was about his cock and his pleasure and his compulsions. Giving in to their terrible sway, he quickly untied the sashes and secured one over her eyes, knotting it tightly behind her head. He forced the second sash between her teeth and yanked it tight, forcing her tongue back and muting her cries.

Don't do this, the last sane bit of his mind urged, but he snuffed the words, the knife quivering in his hand. He stood back and touched its point to her right nipple. Rae stiffened and stilled, finally controlling her impulse to jerk away.

Sam drew the blade over the distended nubbin and in a circle around the areola, power pulsing like liquid heat through his veins. He drew an S and an L on her right breast and a U and a T on her left, pressing hard enough to cause the blood to bead along the letters. Rae jerked and mewled against her gag, her nostrils flaring.

Without thinking what he was doing, or why, he opened his left hand and drew the blade along the fleshy part of his palm, hard enough to draw blood. He sucked in his breath as the sting registered.

Rae was holding onto the chains in a white-knuckled grip. Sam reached for her right hand, prying her fingers loose. Holding her palm open, he pressed the knife blade into the fleshy pad. Rae gurgled against her gag, her entire body trembling. Sam pressed his bleeding palm to hers, as if they were making some kind of sacred pact, sealed with their mingled blood.

Rae's face was pale, her forehead glistening with sweat. Sam knew he'd gone past the line, way past, but he still felt driven by a kind of compulsion he couldn't control. Dropping the knife, he pulled desperately at his pants, dragging them down his thighs and kicking them away.

Grabbing Rae around the waist, he lifted her into his arms and forced her legs around his hips, angling himself so he could fuck her. Her cunt was still wet from the forced orgasm and he pushed himself inside her, groaning at the hot clamp of her velvet muscles around his cock.

He pushed her down and lifted her up, fucking himself with her body. Lust raged through him like an elixir, giving him the strength and stamina of ten men. He plunged in and out of Rae's tight cunt and within minutes he felt the surging rise of his seed exploding deep in Rae's hot, wet embrace.

He held her to him for several moments as his heart slowed its wild pace and his cock softened inside her. Her head had fallen back, her dark hair streaming behind her, the blood dripping in thin lines down her slender frame.

"Christ," he murmured, the spell broken at last, horror replacing the savage lust of just a moment before. "What have I done? What the fuck have I done?"

Chapter 12

She was so pale, sagging heavily against her wrist cuffs, her head lolling back as if her neck was broken. "Rae? Rae!" Sam stood frozen, for a split second thinking somehow he'd killed her! He sagged with relief when he saw the slow rise and fall of her chest.

Springing into action, he pulled the blindfold from her head and unknotted the gag with trembling fingers. Releasing the cuffs with a jerk at the Velcro, he caught her as she sank down. Gathering her into his arms, he stumbled with the dead weight of her limp body toward the bed. He set her as gently as he could onto the mattress.

Bending over her, he pushed the hair from her eyes. Her forehead was damp and clammy. "Rae," he said softly, his voice catching. "Open your eyes."

To his relief, she stirred slightly and her eyes fluttered opened, but only for a second. Her lids closed, a small sigh issuing from her lips as she turned her head away from him. Her body, legs and arms were marked with thin red lines, some of them bleeding, as if she'd fought her way naked through brambles and prickly bushes. The words he'd carved on her breasts and belly were still visible and shame rose inside him like a corrosive acid.

All the mixed-up anger, hurt and lust that had spurred him past his own boundaries had evaporated, leaving behind only the residue of self-loathing and contrition.

"I'm sorry," he whispered, not sure if she could hear him. "I'm sorry."

He ran his finger lightly along some of the cuts, relieved at least to see none of them were deep—they looked worse than they were because of the blood. Except for her palm, which continued to bleed, soaking now into the white sheets where her hand rested. He was vaguely aware of the cut on his own palm, but he didn't care. Rae was what mattered now. What had always mattered.

Forcing himself to be calm, he moved quickly toward her tiny bathroom, where he ran hot water over a washcloth and squeezed it out. He grabbed the first aid kit he kept beneath the sink and returned to Rae. She still hadn't moved, though he was relieved to note her breathing was deeper and more even now—she might just be sleeping, exhausted from the ordeal he'd put her through.

He would clean her cuts as best he could and let her rest. He would provide what aftercare he could, but nothing, he knew, could ever make this right. He'd taken her too far, too fast, and now they would both pay the price.

~*~

Something warm moved over her skin so gently that at first it was part of her dream, the edges between dream and reality a blur. She felt the softness of his breath passing over her cheek, caressing her eyelids.

I'm sorry, I'm sorry...

The words where little more than a sibilant whisper, like the rustle of leaves against the window of her consciousness.

She realized she was lying on her bed. A warm, wet washcloth was moving lightly over her skin, awakening the sting as it washed away the blood...

It all came hurtling back in stark detail—the knife, the jolt of pure terror as he drew the sharp point across her flesh, the blood, bright as death, the chains, the blindfold, the gag thick and dry against her tongue, the sudden sharp stab of pain in her palm, his huge cock impaling her like a sword.

The soft cloth continued to move carefully over her arms and legs. She was fully awake now but kept her eyes closed, her body limp. She let herself be soothed as she drifted, her mind emptying.

I'm sorry, I'm sorry...

The wet cloth was replaced with a dry one, patting along her body. She felt something gooey smeared onto her palm, which throbbed in a steady pulse that matched the rhythm of her heart. She felt the press of something binding the cut closed and then a covering of soft gauze.

I'm sorry, I'm sorry...

She felt the lift in the mattress as he stood. The touch of his lips on her forehead was as light as a father's kiss. The tenderness of it caused something to catch in her throat, but she stayed still, limbs sprawled, lips lightly parted, chest slowly rising and falling.

She lay waiting to hear the click of the padlock as he chained her in place, and then his receding step and light tread on the stairs. Then she could drift back into the dreams where she was flew, free as a bird beneath wide open, sunlit skies.

~*~

Sam stood by her bed for some time, watching her sleep. Rae didn't stir. He was glad, at least, that she was resting. He didn't know how long he stood there, his body heavy, his tortured thoughts bashing themselves like desperate moths against the flame of his regret.

Finally he dragged himself upstairs and into the shower, wishing the hot water could somehow wash away what he'd done. He scrubbed at his palm, wincing as the soap got into the cut, glad for the pain.

He toweled himself dry and went into the bedroom, falling naked onto the sheets. He stared unseeingly out the window, wondering how it had come to this.

It had seemed so perfect at the beginning as he'd spun his devious plan. He'd get the girl he'd been quietly lusting after ever since she'd lain naked and beautiful in this very bed, her eyes bright with need for what he gave her.

He would combine punishment with enlightenment, teaching her to accept her submissive nature. He would bind her closer to him day by day with submersion into her role as his sex slave until it became second nature, until the chains that bound her no longer kept her tethered, but set her free.

But it hadn't worked like that, had it? There were several key elements missing, elements he had chosen to ignore, even though he knew better. Trust. Consent. An exchange of power rather than a forced seizure.

Power corrupts.

He knew that as well as anyone. The relationship was flawed from the start, doomed to failure by its very setup. Relationship? Sam snorted aloud. There was no *relationship*. You couldn't *take* submission; it had to be given. It was a gift, but he'd stolen it, wrested it from her, forced her to hand it over or suffer the consequences. He'd used the guise of punishment for her stealing from him, but his motives had been far more complex.

Absolute power corrupts absolutely.

Sam rolled from the bed and reached for his clothing. He knew what he had to do. And he had to do it now.

~*~

Rae's eyes sprang open at the sound of the basement door opening. She hadn't heard the usual snick of the lock turning. She hadn't heard the intercom with Sam's disembodied voice advising her it was time to get up. The overhead light flicked on and Rae squinted against it, wishing she could sleep some more.

She groaned as she struggled to roll from the bed to the floor to assume the kneeling up position. It didn't feel like morning. Her head hurt and her mouth was sour. Her arms felt heavy when she tried to lift them to clasp her fingers behind her head. She stared down at her right hand. The palm was covered in white gauze, a circle of red at its center where the cut must have seeped. She placed her hands, palms up, on her thighs and hoped he would accept this, given the circumstances.

Sam appeared at the bottom of the stairs carrying something. It took Rae's fogged brain a moment to recognize what it was. Sam had the overnight bag she'd packed with clothes she'd never been permitted to wear.

Moving toward her, he dropped it and stood staring at her, looking for a moment oddly helpless. Then his face closed, his mouth pulling down in a frown. He looked worse than she felt—his blond hair springing up at odd angles from his head, purple smudges of fatigue beneath bloodshot eyes.

"Get up," he ordered. "Don't kneel like that. Stand up."

~ 184 ~

His tone was odd, not angry precisely, but flat, as if she'd done something wrong. Had she done something wrong? Was he going to punish her?

She rose to her feet, wondering if she would be able to grasp her elbows behind her back as she stood at attention, without making the cut on her palm begin to bleed again. She started to try when he stopped her with a hand on her forearm.

"No. Sit down. Sit on the bed, Rae. I don't want you on your knees or at attention."

Thoroughly confused, Rae sat as ordered, tucking her legs beneath her body, making herself small. Sam retrieved the overnight bag and dropped it onto the bed beside her. She stared at it but made no move toward it, as he hadn't given her permission to do so.

He looked at her and then at the bag. He reached for it and unzipped it, rummaging through it a bit before pulling out a pair of underwear, a bra, a blouse and a pair of jeans.

"Get dressed. We need to talk."

Get dressed?

Rae hadn't worn anything in the weeks she'd been in the dungeon, except the corset and stockings he sometimes had her wear for his amusement. Slave girls didn't wear blouses and jeans. Why was he giving her this stuff? It was only day seventeen, wasn't it? Had she miscounted the little balls of tissue hidden in the drawer? Had she somehow lost track of that much time? Were the thirty days actually up?

Sam stood, shoving his hands into his jeans pockets. "Come upstairs when you're dressed. I'll make some coffee."

"Upstairs?" Rae echoed stupidly. What game was he playing at? Was he ordering her to do these things so he could punish her for breaking the rules? Was this a new, elaborate sort of training, the kind where she would fail no matter what and then be taught a lesson?

Without waiting to see if she obeyed, Sam turned on his heel and crossed the room, disappearing up the stairs. She waited to hear the sound of the lock, but didn't even hear the door close. She stared at the clothing and finally reached out to touch the panties.

Again she wondered: what game was he playing?

Still, he'd given her a direct command. *Get dressed.* She knew she'd better obey. And coffee sounded very good at the moment. Maybe there would be food, too. This was the first time he'd allowed her to eat before showering, but nothing about this strange day was usual.

She pulled on her underwear, which didn't rise high enough to cover the word scratched on her stomach.

C-U-N-T.

She knew in her head she should feel outrage at this degradation yet she couldn't seem to muster the emotion. Nor could she deny the tug in her sex and the tingle in her nipples as she stared at her defiled body. She would have liked to take the time to think these odd feelings through, but didn't dare take too much time. Sam was waiting for her.

Gingerly she put on the bra, staring down at the faint trace of letters still visible on her breasts. There were scratches along her arms and legs and actual cuts on her inner thighs and, of course, on the palm hidden by gauze.

She sucked in her breath as she relived the scene in her mind. He'd used a knife, terrifying her, thrilling her, igniting sensations she barely understood. The session had been intense, even brutal. Yet how tenderly he'd ministered to her afterwards, gently cleaning and washing the wounds *he'd* inflicted.

Rae knew she should hate him for what happened, and she did, yes, of course she did. And yet...

And yet, something inside her felt different. Stronger. Newly empowered. She had seen her own blood; she had endured the cut of the blade. In an odd way she felt like some kind of ancient warrior who has been through a rite of passage. She felt a kind of pride, even triumph, that she'd faced it and come out stronger.

She pulled on her jeans and buttoned her blouse. She ran her hands through her tangled hair, wishing she'd had a chance to shower before dressing.

She could smell the aroma of fresh coffee wending its way down the basement stairs. She riffled through the bag and found her shoes, a pair of slip-on flats, which she set on the floor and stepped into. He hadn't said anything about shoes, though. She paused, hesitating, wondering what she should do.

He'd said to get dressed. He'd put the clothing on the bed for her. He hadn't taken out the shoes. She decided to leave them off, instead putting them back into the bag. With a last glance around the dungeon, she hurried up the stairs on bare feet.

As she walked through the living room, following her nose toward the kitchen, she saw to her surprise that it was still dark outside. She'd assumed it must be morning but now realized it must still be night. Why had he got her up in the middle of the night? The sense of disquiet that had fallen over her since he'd first come down the dungeon steps deepened. What the hell was going on?

Sam was standing at the counter pouring the coffee into mugs, his back to her. She couldn't help but admire the broad curve of his shoulders and the way the muscles in his back moved. She stood hesitantly at the door of the kitchen, not sure if she was supposed to kneel on the floor or sit at the table. She cleared her throat and Sam turned toward her. He smiled tightly at her, waving toward the table.

"Sit down." He placed a basket of blueberry muffins on the table and set her mug in front of her. He sat across from her, hunching over his mug, eyes down. She waited, wondering again what he was up to, but too well trained to ask. He usually let her drink her own coffee when he brought down breakfast in the mornings.

Deciding that rule still held, she reached for the cup and took a sip.

"Hungry? Want a muffin?"

Rae stared at the basket, trying to figure out what he wanted. Direct questions, or were they rhetorical? He seemed to be waiting, so she said, "Um, yes, Sir. I am hungry. I would like a muffin."

"So, have one." He gestured toward the basket with his left hand and Rae saw the bandage across it. She flashed back to the scene in the dungeon, to the blood, the sweat, the terror, the pain, the desire...

Had he cut himself too? But why? The world seemed to be tipping around her, the rules changing too fast.

"Oh, I get it." Sam's voice brought her back to the present. "You aren't used to eating by yourself anymore. Well, get used to it. You have my permission to eat on your own. No more feedings. You're going home today."

"Excuse me?" She must have misheard. She thought he'd said she was going home.

"We're done. It's over."

Had she really lost that much track of time?

"It's been thirty days?"

"No, but it doesn't matter. You're going home. I've called a cab. It'll be here in a few minutes."

"A cab? What? I don't understand." She couldn't seem to process whatever it was he was saying. Where were they going in a cab? He had a car. Why didn't he drive? What about her shower? Her grooming? She wanted to crawl back into her bed and sleep some more. Then maybe she'd figure out what was going on.

She glanced toward the oven, noting the time on the small clock there: 3:05 AM. She realized they'd been conversing almost like equals. She hadn't asked permission to speak. This would surely result in punishment later. Deciding not to compound the punishment, Rae asked, "May I speak, Sir"

Sam looked annoyed. "Yes, yes, say whatever you want. And don't call me Sir."

Confused, even a little frightened, Rae continued, "It's the middle of the night. Why are we taking a cab? Where are we going? I don't understand what's going on."

"*We're* not taking a cab. You're. Going. Home." He made each word its own sentence. "We're done. You're getting off with time served, okay? That make it clearer for you?"

Why did he sound so angry? What had she done wrong? Was he really just sending her away? Just like that?

Whatever appetite she'd had was gone. Her stomach felt tight and hard and the coffee tasted bitter in her mouth. She pushed the mug away.

They both turned at the sound of a car horn beeping. "He's here," Sam said, pushing his chair back from the table. "Go get your stuff from the dungeon. I'll get your laptop."

She stared at him. "Go on," he urged. "Hurry up. I'm letting you go. Don't you get it?" The horn beeped again and Sam walked quickly out of the room.

Rae stood slowly. The clothing rubbed at her skin, irritating it. She heard the sound of the front door being pulled open, and Sam calling out that they'd be just a second. For some reason her legs felt like lead, but she forced them to move, to carry her back through the living room and down the basement stairs.

She gathered her toothbrush and other items from the bathroom and stuffed them into the bag. She found the shoes and slipped them onto her feet as she hoisted the bag over her shoulder.

With a last quick glance around the dungeon, she hurried toward the stairs.

Sam was standing in the front hall, Rae's briefcase in his hand, her laptop case slung over his shoulder. As she approached, he opened the front door and walked out into the night.

Rae hesitated on the threshold. Though it was still summer, there was a coolness in the air, a hint of the autumn to come. She looked up at the stars, a million diamond pinpricks in the black velvet of the sky.

When Sam turned back to look at her, she forced herself to step out into the night, following Sam down the walkway to the yellow cab waiting at the curb. Was this really happening?

Sam pulled the car door open and swung her things into the backseat. As she approached he took her bag from her and deposited that as well. He pressed something into her hand and she realized it was her cell phone.

Reality settled over her, heavy as stone. He was sending her away. She had dreamed of this moment a dozen times or more. She was being released from the dungeon! So why wasn't she filled with joy, ecstatic to be free at last? She would never have to see his face again, never have to feel the hard crack of his hand on her ass, the cut of the cane, the hot leather stroke of the flogger, the relentless vibration of the wand at her clit, the full feeling of his hard cock moving inside her...

"Go on," he said softly. "Go."

He pushed gently at her shoulder, forcing her down into the backseat of the cab. Leaning into the open window of the driver's door, he gave him Rae's address and handed him a wad of money.

"Wait just a moment, if you will."

Sam stepped back and, reaching into his pocket, pulled out something and handed it through Rae's open window. It was a piece of paper. Rae took it, though it was too dark to see what was written there. She half expected him to tell her to get out now — the game was over, she'd either passed or failed whatever test he'd devised.

But he said nothing. He really was sending her away. She realized with something approaching shock that she didn't want to go! She didn't want to never see him again. How could she stop whatever was happening now?

"What about the money?" she blurted. "The money I owe you? Don't we have to work out terms?"

"Excuse me," he said, speaking to the driver. "Can you turn on the light for the lady?" The driver obliged. "Read it," Sam ordered.

Rae looked down at the page she held in her hands. It was the indemnity agreement they'd written together, absolving her of any wrong doing, noting the *loan* of $133,000 made with Sam's full knowledge and consent. Across the sheet in big red letters were the words: PAID IN FULL, with Sam's bold, slanted signature beneath it.

"Take care, Rae," he said softly. Then he turned away.

Chapter 13

Rae stood for a long moment just inside her door. Her apartment was a single, large room, partitioned by carved wooden dividers that created the illusion of a separate bedroom, office space and galley kitchen. Along with her desk and filing cabinet, she'd furnished the apartment with plump, comfortable sofas and a big leather recliner where she liked to watch TV. The kitchen table was a fifties throwback she'd found at an estate sale, complete with a red Formica top and matching padded chairs with chrome legs.

There was a thin veneer of dust on everything and the air was close and still. She'd only been away for a few weeks, yet the place looked somehow abandoned, frozen in time. Dropping her bags, she moved toward the living room window to let in the fresh night air.

Sinking down into the recliner, she glanced at the wall clock. It was nearly five in the morning. The rising sun was already painting the city gray and lavender, with brushes of gold outlining the skyline. Though she was bone weary, Rae knew she wouldn't sleep. Her head was so crowded, it was standing room only.

Reaching for the remote, she turned on the TV. She realized she hadn't heard the news for over two weeks.

She hadn't checked her email—Sam had done it for her, reading to her what he considered important and allowing her to dictate her replies. She hadn't seen her snail mail—it was being held for her at the apartment manager's office until her "return from Japan". She hadn't been shopping or walked the streets of Manhattan, or been to a movie or read a book. She hadn't even fed herself or used a razor on her own. She hadn't worn makeup or used her blow dryer or plucked her eyebrows or bought a new lipstick. She hadn't worked on drumming up new clients or even done any work for *Ryker Solutions* beyond a few brief consultations with Sam on the *Ichi* deal.

Rae flicked off the TV, aware she had no idea what was on the screen. What the hell was the matter with her? She should be dancing for joy, leaping around the apartment calling, "Free at last! Free at last! Thank God Almighty, free at last!"

So why did she feel so empty?

The thought made her realize she was, in fact, empty. She hadn't touched the muffins he'd put on the table. She hadn't eaten since their lunch the day before—chicken salad and wedges of crisp apple, shared with Sam.

After she'd gotten used to being fed, she'd come to enjoy their meals together. Sam always let her eat her fill, alternating bites with her, watching her to see if she enjoyed it. He seemed to take satisfaction in her pleasure and he really was quite a good cook. She, on the other hand, could burn water. Frozen microwave dinners and takeout were more her speed, when she remembered to eat at all.

Sam had forced her to slow down—to taste the food, to savor the moment. He would even pat her chin and wipe her lips afterwards with a napkin, almost like a father for his child, though it had never felt like that at the time. There had been a certain sensual element to the meals, something she'd certainly never experienced before. Something, she admitted now, that she quite liked.

Pushing herself from the recliner, Rae walked into the tiny kitchen and pulled open the small refrigerator. There were some condiments in the door and a lone bottle of tonic water on the shelf next to a tub of margarine. Sam had cleared out the perishables, she recalled now, not that there had been that much to start with.

Along with two trays of ice cubes, the freezer contained a blob of freezer-burned meat that was probably chicken, and a box of spinach, both items, she now recalled, she'd bought with the intent to make a homemade meal, though clearly that had never come to fruition.

She shut the door with a sigh and turned toward the pantry cabinet, where she found box of crackers and some Cheese Whiz. There was also a bottle of premium vodka with a good four inches remaining.

"Food for the gods," she murmured, taking the items, including the vodka, from the cabinet and carrying them to the table. Grabbing a paper plate, she tore open the one remaining packet of crackers in the box and dumped some on the plate.

She winced with pain as she pulled at the cap on the Cheese Whiz can, the cut on her palm suddenly reminding her of their last bizarre session in the dungeon. Her snack for the moment forgotten, she held out her right hand and carefully pulled back the gauze held in place by paper tape.

Beneath the butterfly bandage, she could see the cut was only about an inch long but it looked deep. She found herself wondering if it would leave a scar—a ridged reminder of when she had been Sam's sex slave. Again that curious sense of pride moved through her as she stared at the wound. It was like a badge of courage—a reminder of what she'd been through.

She reached absently for her collar, stroking the stiff leather with practiced fingers. Her slave collar! Why the hell was she still wearing it? Standing, she hurried into the bathroom and flicked on the light, positioning herself in front of the mirrored medicine cabinet that hung over the sink.

She stared for a long time at her face. The angular planes of cheekbone and jaw were softened, making her look closer to nineteen than twenty-nine. Her skin was clear, a natural blush of soft pink on her cheeks instead of the tan foundation she had applied as part of a full makeup regime every day, whether staying home or going out. *Must be all that fresh fruit and meat he gives me*, she thought with an inward grin, *not to mention the constant orgasms*, before her mind had a chance to form the thought in past tense.

Before the dungeon, she used to spend at least an hour after each shower, carefully drying and styling her hair into a sleek, smooth curtain of dark satin. As often as not, she'd sweep it back in a French twist, thinking this gave her a more formidable, serious presence in the business world. Now as she stared at her reflection, her hair looked thick and unruly, falling in a tumble of waves around her face.

Beyond the physical changes her time with Sam had wrought, there was something else—something in her expression as she gazed back at herself, almost a kind of inward smile, the enigmatic smile of someone who has a secret. A good secret.

She touched the collar again as she stared at herself. She was so used to wearing it that she only thought about it when Sam used the ring to tether her in place, or when he removed it so she could shower. She herself had never been permitted to take it off. It was, he would remind her, a sign of his ownership.

"Well," she said, trying to make her voice bright in the stillness of her apartment. "I'm a free woman now."

Opening the medicine cabinet, she found a box of bandages and a tube of antibiotic ointment. Without removing the butterfly bandage, she squirted a bit of the ointment along the edges and taped a new, fresh gauze pad over the cut. As she worked, her thoughts veered back to the Sam's careful aftercare following the knife session.

She'd actually passed out at some point during the intense session, her mind and body shifting into sensory overload as a result of all he was doing to her. When she came to, she was in her bed, with Sam carefully washing her body and patting her dry. She'd lain still with her eyes closed, not wanting him to realize she was conscious, afraid he'd stop taking care of her if he knew.

I'm sorry, I'm sorry...

His words drifted back to her now, uttered with the pained conviction of a broken heart. At the time she'd been so focused on what had just happened — the knife, the blood, the terror, the tenderness of his aftercare — that she'd barely processed those words or their meaning.

All at once she understood. He hadn't let her go because of something she'd done wrong. He'd let her go because of what *he'd* done wrong. The realization should have filled her with vindicated satisfaction, but it only left her feeling even more bereft than before.

Reaching behind her neck, she fingered the buckle of the slave collar and pushed the leather strap through it. She pulled the collar free and dropped it into the sink. She put her hand on her throat, lightly wrapping her fingers around it, as Sam sometimes did when he stared into her eyes.

Her nipples perked in response to the memory and she dropped her hand, confused by her reaction. She reminded herself she was hungry.

Returning to the kitchen, she retrieved the bottle of tonic from the fridge and got out a glass from the cabinet. She added ice cubes and poured in plenty of vodka. Though she wasn't in the habit of drinking hard liquor at six in the morning, she gave herself permission. She'd just been through two weeks of pure hell. She was celebrating her freedom.

She blinked away the sudden tears, telling herself they were from fatigue.

The food tasted surprisingly good, the crunchy buttery flavor of the crackers nicely offset by the gooey, salty cheese spread. She ate a few off the plate and took a healthy swig of the strong drink she'd prepared herself. The tonic was flat, but better than nothing. She wished she had some fresh lime.

She finished the crackers and cheese and stood from the table, wondering what to do next. She drifted aimlessly around her small apartment, straightening a picture on the wall, running her finger over the spines of the books in the narrow built-in cases on either side of the TV, stopping to stare out the window at the play of color against the buildings as the sun edged upward into the summer sky.

She reached again to finger her collar, but it wasn't there. Her neck felt oddly naked without it. At the same time, her clothes felt constricting, the underwire of her bra cutting into her ribcage. She kicked off her flats and unbuttoned her blouse, pulling it off. Reaching behind herself, she unclasped the hooks of her bra and shrugged it off with a grateful sigh. Undoing her jeans, she slipped out of them, dragging her underwear along with the pants.

That felt better. It was good to be naked. It felt right somehow. Again she put her hand on her throat, feeling the lack there. She finished the vodka and tonic, letting its warmth move through her chest and loosen the stranglehold of tension she held in her gut.

Without taking too much time to examine her motives, she returned to the bathroom and reached for the slave collar. Pushing her hair back, she buckled it around her neck and look defiantly at herself in the mirror.

Maybe now she could sleep.

~*~

Sam awoke with a start, disoriented and confused. He looked around and realized he had fallen asleep in the dungeon, on Rae's bed. He reached for his cock, which was erect from lingering dreams involving Rae naked and bent over in the stocks, her back arched, legs spread, her ass a lovely cherry red from a recent paddling, the skin hot to the touch.

He stroked himself, letting the images play out. He loved the little grunts and sighs he pulled from her with the lash of the whip, almost indistinguishable from the gasps of pleasure when he fingered her cunt until she begged for permission to come. He loved the way the skin on her chest and throat mottled, the coins of color rising on her cheeks when she neared orgasm.

"Please, Sir, oh please! May I come…" That breathy, sweet entreaty and her pout of frustration when he denied her.

He pulled at his cock, wishing it was her hot, wet mouth instead of his hand moving over his shaft. If she were here now, he would have her lie on the edge of the bed, her head hanging just off the mattress. Standing in front of her, he would lower his cock into her mouth, not stopping until she'd taken the full length of it. Gripping her head on either side, he would ease himself in and out, urging her to take it, to surrender herself fully to him while he fucked her mouth.

He loved not only the warm, enfolding clutch of her tongue and throat muscles against his throbbing cock, but also the exhilarating rush of power he got from using her in that way. She became his vessel, the place where his cock went. She existed at that moment solely to pleasure him, to serve him, to submit to his whim and his lust.

He stroked himself faster, closing his eyes and letting himself pant. The sheet fell over the side of his face as he shifted and for a moment he thought it was Rae's silky hair. He pressed his nose into the soft, lingering scent of her skin on the sheets as he pushed himself toward a climax. He came suddenly, several small, shuddering, unsatisfying spurts of spunk onto his stomach.

He lay there a while before reaching for the edge of the sheet to wipe it away. Had she been there, he would have had her lick it up. No. Had she been there, he wouldn't have been jerking himself off.

He looked around the room, the place that had been Rae's world since he'd brought her home. She'd spent all her time in the dungeon, save for the occasional trip to his office, where for the most part he'd kept her on her knees between his legs.

Why had he never brought her up to his bed?

Because she was a sex slave, that's why. She was there to be punished, not adored. And he'd punished her, all right. He'd knocked that sassy, willful arrogance right out of her. He'd molded her into a willing, compliant slave girl, all in the space of a few steady weeks of constant stimulation, training and erotic pain. He'd even had notions of making her his permanent slave girl, bound not by the terms of his blackmail, but by mutual consent and desire.

What a joke. His own secret longing had blinded him to the truth. She'd brought him sharply back to reality, that was for damn sure. The venom in her tone when she'd snarled: *There is no us.* She'd just been playing the game, pretending to submit, doing her time. And who could blame her?

He'd been so sure of himself and of her — telling himself she was only denying her true impulses, rejecting them because they didn't fit into her image of herself as a modern, independent woman. Under the guise of the thirty-day punishment, he'd planned to show her the potential power of true submission. He'd been confident he would be able to guide her and train her to accept and embrace her true nature.

Arrogant bastard. Who the fuck did he think he was?

Letting her go was the one right thing he'd done since this whole mess started. He would move on, put her out of his mind.

"If I never see Rae Johansen again, it will be too soon," he said aloud to the empty room. Even before the words were out of his mouth, he knew they were a lie.

~*~

Rae woke up with her fingers buried in her cunt, the scent of her own sex ripe in the air. She let her legs fall open, lingering on the sensual feelings brought out by the dream that was already fading from her memory.

As she came fully awake, she jerked her hand away with a small cry and reached for the sheets. Sam might be watching on his closed-circuit TV! He'd punish her with a trip to the cage for touching herself. She hated the cage, hated being left there and ignored, unable to move or get comfortable until he decided she'd had enough.

Then she remembered.

She wasn't in the dungeon. She was home, alone, free. She could touch herself as much as she wanted.

There was no one watching, no one who gave a damn if she came without permission, or if she came at all.

Licking her fingers, she returned her hand to her pussy, ignoring the light throb of the cut on her palm, determined to rub herself to orgasm. It was *her* cunt, *her* body. She could do whatever the fuck she wanted.

She closed her eyes and willed the image of Johnny Depp, so sexy as the anti-hero in *The Libertine*, his liquid brown eyes mesmerizing her as his hand moved, buried in her crotch beneath her silk and taffeta as they rode toward London in their carriage…but it was Sam's face she saw, with his blue-grey eyes flashing as he commanded her to come… *Come for me…do it… now…*

She is bent facedown over the padded sawhorse, a butt plug nestled fully inside her, the Hitachi wand whirring at her spread cunt. Her nipples throb from the clover clamps, weighted with lead teardrops. The wand is removed. She feels a lubricated dildo pressing its way inside her, sliding against the plug buried in her ass, separated only by the thin membrane between anus and cunt.

The wand returns, sending vibrations in concentric circles radiating from her clit into her full orifices, making her shake as the orgasm rises. She's been tethered to the sawhorse for hours, teased nearly to orgasm again and again, always denied at the last second. This time, she knows, she won't be able to hold back.

Don't stop, she begs silently, don't stop.

He doesn't stop, but keeps moving the ball of the wand in teasing circles over her labia, flicking it lightly across her clit until she is panting and nearly faint with need.

"Please, Sir, may I come?"

Rae dropped her hand, her orgasm receding in the shock of realization at what she'd just done. Though he'd set her free, or if she were going to be more honest about it, kicked her out, Rae had just begged the man she was supposed to despise for permission to come. The man who had cut her with a knife, who had carved demeaning words on her body, who had raped her while she was bound and gagged.

Stop it, she told herself. *Don't dwell on it. It's over. You're free.*

If it felt like she'd been abandoned and kicked unceremoniously to the curb, it was only some kind of weird Stockholm Syndrome reaction. She'd been conditioned to crave what he offered, trained on a diet of constant stimulation and deprivation. She wasn't yet herself. She just needed time to recover. Time to put him and the whole sordid ordeal behind her.

She would start fresh. She would reinvent herself in a new city, maybe a new state! There was nothing and no one holding her in Manhattan. She'd burned every bridge. She was well and truly alone. And that was fine. Rae Johansen needed no one to feel complete. She was better off on her own. She didn't need some man telling her when to pee, when to come, when to eat, when to think.

If she never saw Sam Ryker again, it would be too soon.

Rolling to her side, she ignored the trickle of tears sliding onto the sheets. Pulling the pillow over her head, she waited for exhaustion to pull her into sleep.

Chapter 14

Rae touched her collar, which for some reason she still hadn't removed. She'd even worn it when she went out for groceries and no one had batted an eye. This was, after all, Manhattan.

Opening her laptop, she went to her email, just in case he'd written.

Nothing.

She herself had typed several emails to Sam, hitting delete each time, the words all wrong. She told herself she should just let it go. Move on and put Sam Ryker and the whole strange experience from her mind.

She tried to tell herself he was a power hungry madman, a sadistic bastard who had blackmailed her into submission, but she knew that wasn't true. Maybe at first he'd just been intent on getting revenge, but things had shifted between them. She wasn't entirely sure how or when the change began, but it was real. And she couldn't forget it. Her age-old tactic of stuffing things down and ignoring them was no longer working.

She could still hear his voice, ragged with pain and emotion as he tended to her cuts after the dangerous knife play. *I'm sorry. I'm sorry.* As odd as it was, even to her own ears, she'd fallen in love with him in that moment and she had no idea what to do about it.

It was that man she needed to reach, to tell. Even if she couldn't have him, Rae felt she owed Sam at least something of the truth. Girding her courage, she tried again.

From: Rae.Johansen@RykerSolutions.net
To: Samuel.Ryker@RykerSolutions.net
Subject: Sir

I don't really know how to begin, so I guess I'll do my usual and just dive right in, leaping before I look. When this whole thing started, I mean, when you busted me and offered your terms, I figured this was just your perverted way of getting into my pants again. You had backed me against the wall. I felt I had little choice.

Before I say anything else, I want to say how sorry I am that I stole from you, that I didn't trust you enough to seek another solution. I can't undo that, but I still plan to pay you back, no matter what else happens (or doesn't) between us.

Back to these past weeks. I hated you at first, Sam. I guess you knew that, as I didn't try to hide it. I was shocked and terrified to be held in your dungeon, chained and at your mercy. My god, who wouldn't be? I've had a lot of time to think things over, both when you left me alone in the dungeon, and these past two days since I've been back at my place.

One thing I've realized is I have spent my whole life running as fast as I can to get away from myself. I know that sounds odd, but it's true. I think somehow I figured if I kept moving, accomplishing things, making my way in the big bad world on my own, I wouldn't have to slow down and realize how lonely I was, or that I really had no idea what I wanted or needed in my life.

I've never been in a committed relationship, not one where I really gave of myself, where I allowed myself to be vulnerable. I went to a shrink for a while in my early twenties—trying to figure out why I was unable to really click with anyone. Why I never felt that rush, that thrill that my girlfriends all seemed to feel when in the throes of a new relationship. The therapy didn't go too far—I felt like I was being lectured and I just bagged it. I told myself I was too strong a woman to fall in love. Love was for weaklings, for women who needed to lean on a man to feel complete.

I never told the therapist I felt broken inside. Is that the right word? Like there was a connection missing, something that caused a short circuit every time I got close to a real feeling, to being vulnerable.

When we went out that time last year, the one time, the circuit was completed, maybe for the first time in my life. You told me I was hiding from my own feelings when I rejected the bondage and dominance you offered, and my reactions to it. I told you that you were just egocentric and used to getting whatever you wanted with a woman, and that we'd be better off being just friends and business associates.

But the truth was, I was terrified. Which is ironic, given that I'd always been seeking that kind of intensity of connection. But when you appeared, offering it, I ran for the hills! My therapist would have said it was me denying my real feelings so I could continue to stay safe from getting hurt. I was like this person encased in an impenetrable plastic bubble. Nobody was going to get in, period.

These past few weeks—I don't know how to say this, but you managed to find a way in. I'm honestly not sure anyone could have reached me, not the way you have. Yes, your measures were drastic, even extreme. And yes, I know I'm supposed to be outraged and horrified at what you did to me—keeping me chained and enslaved, using me like an object, your personal property, your sex slave...

I *was* outraged and horrified. That wasn't an act. But beneath it. OMG, Sam, beneath it, you were finally, for the first time, piercing the bubble I spent a lifetime building around my heart and soul. You reached me, that secret, vulnerable little girl place inside where I hide my true feelings and needs. You pulled away the curtains and tore down the walls.

You brought out feelings and desires I never knew I possessed. You showed me, whether you meant to or not, that at my core I am submissive. That I need what you gave me. I long for it. I miss it.

I want it back.

Remember when I said there was no *us*? I was lying. For the first time, I find I am part of an "us", or at least I was, for those few weeks we spent together.

And now it's gone.

And here I sit. Alone again, not sure how to find my way back to what I used to be. Knowing in my heart I don't really want to.

Rae stared at what she'd written, not ready to send it, but not quite willing to delete it either. Without hitting the send button, she logged out of her email and closed the laptop lid.

Once over lunch when they were first working together, Sam had made the observation that the world moved so fast now, no one had time to just sit down and write a letter by hand. Everything was instant, composed in a flash and sent with a press of the finger on a keyboard. Rae had said, wasn't that a good thing? Sam had nodded that yes, he supposed it was, but didn't she think that sometimes, something handwritten on real paper made more of an impact? Forced us to slow down, at least a little? At the time she'd shrugged this off, but now she understood.

She glanced out the window — it was still light out, still time for what she wanted to do. She dressed in jeans and a blouse, not even bothering with makeup, which would have been inconceivable before her time with Sam. Grabbing her keys, wallet and cell phone in case he called, she left her apartment, a woman on a mission. Down her block was a small stationery store, sandwiched between a dry cleaners and a deli. It was an old-fashioned mom-and-pop kind of place that had somehow managed to survive, despite the incursion of superstores.

She breathed in the dry, musty scent of paper and ink as she moved along the narrow aisles cluttered with office supplies. She stopped at the stationery section, looking over the selection. Underneath boxes of thank you and get well soon cards, she found what she was looking for—a box of pale ecru bond paper with a dark blue edge. It came with matching envelopes, the inside of each envelope the same blue as the stationery's borders.

She searched the pen section for a long time before finally spying what she wanted in a dusty box on a top shelf. It was a fountain pen, black with a silver nib, and came with a few ink cartridges. It cost quite a bit more than she'd expected to pay, but she decided it was worth it. She made her purchase and returned to her apartment.

Sitting at her desk, she took the pen from the bag and spent a few minutes placing the ink cartridge inside it and testing it out on a cheap piece of printer paper. She practiced writing her name until the ink flowed smoothly. It was a rich, royal blue. She realized it had been some time since she'd used a pen, any pen, for much more than grocery lists or the occasional check. She liked the feel of this fine pen, its solid weight and smooth nib lending a kind of loftiness, an importance, to her words.

Rae opened the box of stationery and drew out a single sheet. She lay it flat on the desk and began to write.

~*~

Sam lifted his head at the sound of the mail chute opening in his front door and the soft thud of the day's mail hitting the floor. He still hadn't returned to his Manhattan office. He knew he needed to get back there, to at least pretend to a return to his old life, but he hadn't yet found the will.

He glanced at his watch. It was nearly five o'clock on Monday evening, time to call it a day, he supposed, though he hadn't accomplished much.

Sam recognized he was a man given to obsession. He would become fixated on a project, working sometimes twenty hours out of twenty-four to bring an idea to fruition. In the past, however, this fixation had always been confined to his work. No woman had ever occupied so much space and time in his head before. Or his heart.

That was the damned thing of it. If he could extract and untangle his heart from the whole messy situation, he was sure he could move on and forget Rae. When he'd first made the bizarre deal with her, he hadn't bargained on his emotions getting in the way of his cock or his whip arm. He'd thought he could keep them neatly locked away while he exacted his revenge.

But somehow Rae had managed to get under his skin in a way no one had managed to before. What was it about her that had changed in the short time they'd been together? Or maybe he was asking the wrong question. What was it about himself that had changed?

He knew of course. He'd known it for some time, maybe even from the beginning. He'd been in love with Rae for a long time. But it had been too hard to admit, too much to deal with. So instead he'd focused on his baser emotions, pushing her too far, denying his true feelings in order to keep the pain of her inevitable rejection at bay.

He'd known sending her away would hurt at first, but he hadn't expected the unrelenting enormity of it.

He thought he knew all the different kinds of heartbreak but this was a new one, a crushing sadness, an appalling knowledge of lost chances. The pain was atomic, quite a surprise really.

It had been five days since he'd hustled her into that cab and sent her away. Five days since he'd tasted her lips, felt the warmth of her cunt enveloping his cock, seen the spark of fire and passion in those cobalt blue eyes.

A small bell sounded on his laptop, signaling that an email had arrived. Sam opened his email without any real expectation — probably just another spam.

It was from Rae! His hand shook as he opened the email and began to read…

I don't really know how to begin, so I guess I'll do my usual and just dive right in, leaping before I look…

He read the email a dozen times or more, pondering it, interpreting it, revising his interpretation, letting hope bloom and then wilt, crafting responses, only to delete them a moment later.

Deciding he'd return to it when his emotions had calmed down some, he pushed himself to his feet and walked toward the front door, where a pile of junk mail lay waiting for him. He grabbed it, glancing unenthusiastically through the catalogs and bills, when his eye was caught by an envelope addressed by hand in a pretty, neat cursive, decidedly feminine.

Carrying the whole pile to the living room, he sat down on the sofa and, discarding the rest beside him, turned the envelope over in his hands, studying it. There was no return address. It could just be a ploy to get him to open it — probably just another appeal for money for this charity or that, with the hopes that something handwritten would get his attention.

Well, if that was the case, it had worked. He slipped his thumb beneath the seal on the back of the envelope and opened it. He drew out the single page inside and unfolded it.

Sir,

I want to come back.

The time we spent these past weeks is the first time I have ever felt truly alive. I know that wasn't what you planned, and certainly not what I expected. I have spent my life running so fast so I wouldn't have to stop and take stock of who and what I was. I'm ready to stop running.

If I learned one thing from you, it's to slow down, take a deep breath, let it flow, and really feel what I feel.

I understand you may not want me back. It's a chance I have no choice but to take.

I will be at your doorstep on Monday evening at 6:00. If you are willing to take me back, just open the door. If you are not, do nothing. I will accept your decision and you won't hear from me again.

Your slave girl, Rae

Chapter 15

Rae knelt on the stoop, the collar in her hands. The flagstones were hard beneath her bare knees. Her hair fell into her face but she didn't move. There were two minutes to go until six. Taking a deep breath, she let it out slowly and began to count.

One...two...three...breathe...

She resisted the urge to look up when she heard the lock sliding open and the sound of the door pulling open. *Sixty-five, sixty-six, sixty-seven...*

Her heart skipped a beat and then settled into a rapid anticipatory patter but she managed to hold her position, eyes downcast, arms raised in offering.

She heard him step out onto the stoop. She saw his boots appear in her line of vision. If she bent just a little farther, she could have kissed them. Before she could think further on this, to her vast surprise Sam knelt in front of her.

"Rae."

She looked up into his face, half afraid of what she would see there. There was a question in his eyes, as his lips formed a hesitant smile. When she smiled back, he reached for her, placing his hands on her shoulders.

They knelt there like statues for several long moments. Rae had never felt so aware of him—his strength, his vulnerability. There was a tension between them, vibrating in the stillness.

Sam looked down at the collar she still clutched. Letting go of her, he reached for it and she let him take it. She held her breath expectantly, silently urging him, nodding her head ever so slightly in encouragement.

When he nodded back, Rae lifted her hair from the back of her neck, closing her eyes. When she felt the smooth, stiff leather being placed against her throat, something she'd been clenching tight inside eased a little. When the collar was buckled around her throat, she let the tears she'd been holding back roll down her cheeks.

~*~

Sam held out his hand and Rae took it, allowing him to help her rise. He led Rae into the house, feeling almost as if they were in some kind of dream. A dream that would melt away if he reached too suddenly for it. He held out his arms and she stepped into them, resting her head against his chest. He lifted her chin, his mouth seeking hers. He kissed her, hesitantly at first, though soon with a rising passion. She kissed him back, her ardor equaling his.

Finally they stepped apart, both breathing hard. "How I missed you, Rae," he said. She looked so beautiful, her hair falling loosely about her shoulders, her skin soft and dewy, her eyes shining, her nipples tenting the silky white fabric of her blouse.

She smiled shyly. "Please say you won't send me away again."

The words cut him to the bone. He took her by the shoulders and looked deep into her eyes. "Listen, Rae. I sent you away, not because of anything you did, but because of what *I* was doing. What I was becoming. I took something that should be beautiful and I perverted it to get back at you, to exact revenge.

"I'm not going to lie and say it was all about the money either—it wasn't. It was about that one night we spent, and the way you sent me away, rejecting what I knew was in both our hearts. Instead of being a man, instead of trying to understand and to reach you, I just let it, and you, go. When I had the chance to get you back with blackmail, I seized on it. What I did was no better than stealing, Rae. You stole money—I stole your trust and freedom."

Rae nodded and even though it hurt, Sam found himself grateful for the acknowledgment. She wasn't going to try and gloss over what he'd done. But she was here. She'd returned to him when she could just as easily have turned her back forever.

Sam took Rae's hand and led her into the living room. "I have to admit, until I got your email and the beautiful letter, I didn't think you'd ever want to come back here. I promise you this time will be different. The basis of this kind of relationship—of Dom and sub, of

Master and slave—is trust. I tried to demand it of you, without giving it to you in return. I'm sorry, Rae. You seem to be ready to trust me now, and I'm grateful for that, though frankly I'm not sure I deserve it. Not yet, anyway." He offered a wan smile.

Rae smiled back, though her eyes were suddenly sad. "I appreciate that, Sam. I really do. And by the same token, I hope I can earn your trust again as well."

Sam reached for her once more. He could feel the soft yield of her breasts against his chest as he pulled her close. He moved his hands over her back and lower, finding and cupping her ass. He pulled at the skirt, lifting it so he could feel her skin. "Spread your legs," he ordered softly, pleased when she immediately obeyed. He found the cleft of her sex, already wet and swollen for him, as it should be. He ran his fingers over her labia, satiny smooth to the touch.

"I want you," he murmured, letting her go. "I've thought of little else since you left."

"Me too," she whispered shyly.

"Are you ready to start where we left off?"

Rae glanced toward the basement door and back at Sam. "Yes, Sir. I'm ready."

"We're not going down into the dungeon. We're going upstairs." Her saw her initial confusion and then the slight nod of understanding and the whisper of a smile.

Taking her hand, he walked with her up the stairs to the bedroom. The room was shimmery in the light of candles he'd lit just before going outside to see if she was really waiting there for him, as the letter had promised. He had pulled back the bedding and attached leather straps to the four posters of the bed, cuffs at the ready to secure his slave girl.

"Are you ready to show me you're really mine?"

"Yes, Sir."

"Take off your clothes and lie down on the bed, arms over your head, legs spread. I want to inspect my property."

He felt the tremor run through her body at his words. She had offered herself to him. She had signed that beautiful handwritten letter with the words: *your slave girl*. Was it more than just pretty words? He ached to find out.

He watched as she unbuttoned her blouse, recalling that first day when he'd brought her home for her punishment. Then her face had been flushed with embarrassment, her reluctance evident with every move. Now, though he could see she was nervous, she seemed determined.

Pushing the blouse from her shoulders, she revealed her round, perfect breasts and jutting nipples. She unzipped and stepped out of her skirt and lay across his bed, assuming the position he'd dictated.

She lifted her hips slightly, offering herself to him. Sam's cock was rock hard in his jeans. He pulled his T-shirt over his head and stripped himself naked, though he planned to wait to take his own direct pleasure.

The tip of her little pink tongue ran over her top lip as she gazed at his erect cock with raw desire. "Show respect, slave girl," he said, though he was barely able to keep the grin off his face. Yes, he did want a true slave girl, respectful, submissive and yielding to his will, but he couldn't deny being pleased at her obvious appreciation. There was time, plenty of time, he hoped, to train her in proper decorum.

Sitting on the bed beside her, he ran his fingers over her smooth pubic mound, sliding them down between her spread legs. She moaned softly as he probed her labia, lightly teasing and pulling the silky soft flesh. He felt her heat. She was wet and his cock twitched in anticipation.

Not yet, he told himself. *Not yet.*

He stood and moved to the head of the bed. Taking each wrist, he cuffed her to the posts at the headboard and then did the same thing with her ankles, leaving her spread eagle and vulnerable, his for the taking.

He reached for his single tail whip. He ran the single, deceptively soft strand of leather lightly over her breasts and belly, drawing a shudder from her.

"What are you, Rae?"

"Your slave girl, Sir."

"Who do you belong to?"

"You, Sir."

"Whose cunt is that?"

"Yours, Sir."

"Whose ass?"

"Yours, Sir."

"Whose breasts?"

"Yours, Sir."

"And what can I do with my property?"

"Anything you want, Sir."

Sam nodded, a surge of lust shooting through his cock. "That's right. Anything I want." He drew the whip down her body, pulling it so the tip ran lightly over her labia. "I could whip you until you bleed, isn't that right, slave girl?"

Again she shuddered, and her voice was less steady, but she said, "Yes, Sir."

He drew back the whip with a flick of his wrist, noting her face as she squeezed her eyes shut in sudden anticipation. He lowered the whip without striking her. "Don't anticipate, Rae. Just accept it. All of it. Everything I give you." He stroked her arm and bent down to kiss her cheek.

"You're doing good. Real good," he murmured. "I'm proud of you."

She opened her eyes and smiled.

He sat beside her, cupping her left breast. He reached for her nipple, flicking it lightly until it hardened. He gripped it and twisted, drawing a sudden gasp of pain from her lips.

"Accept it," he repeated. "Everything I give you. Breathe deep. Flow with the pain. Give in to what you long to be. And let me be the one to take you there, not by the hair, but by the hand. Do you want that, Rae? To give yourself freely to me?"

"Yes." She held the s, letting it hiss into a sigh.

"Breathe," he whispered, his fingers still tight on her nipple. He watched with awe and admiration as her face transformed, the tension easing from her features, her eyes slowly opening to focus on his. He twisted again. She let out a rush of air, but kept her eyes on his.

Releasing her tortured nipple, he bent over and put his mouth on it, licking away the pain as he sucked the engorged bud, pebbly hard against his lips. Unable to resist, he kissed and suckled her other nipple as well, enjoying her sweet moans.

He sat up and stared down at the mounds of soft flesh, the nipples like dark pink gumdrops. "One day, when you're properly trained and ready, I'll pierce your nipples. You will take the needle for me, won't you, Rae?" He knew what he was asking. He waited.

She swallowed hard, a flush rising on her cheeks, but she nodded, whispering, "Yes, Sir."

He smiled and stroked her cheek. "Don't worry, sweetheart. That won't happen until you're ready, until you tell me it's what you want."

"Yes, Sir," she repeated.

He ran the whip lightly over her body again, moving in an easy, soothing rhythm until she was fully relaxed and open to him. He caught her off guard with a sudden flick to her right nipple. Rae cried out, jerking in her restraints. Sam reached for her pussy, sliding a finger easily into her wetness.

"Your body doesn't lie, Rae. You need this."

He flicked the second nipple and then focused lower, letting the leather curl around each thigh, leaving small red marks where the tip hit. He struck her bare pubic mound, flicking the tip in quick succession, covering her skin with little blossoms of color, each petal drawn with the tip of his whip.

Rae was writhing in her constraints, her eyes closed, her lips parted. Sam thought about ordering her to open her eyes, to focus directly on the whip, but decided to let her be for now. This didn't have to be training—it was more about reconnecting. He would help center her again, recreate the intricate patterns of pleasure and pain in her nerve endings, remind her body and her soul of what she needed—of what they both needed.

When he struck her labia with the light but direct flick of the whip, Rae gasped and stiffened. "Breathe," he reminded her. "You can do this. You are doing it. For me. For *us*."

Sam couldn't help but recall the last time he'd said those words, and her scathing response. He waited now, holding his breath. Rae slowly opened her eyes and fixed them on his.

"Yes," she finally said. "For *us*. I want this. For us."

Hiding the relief that left him nearly weak, Sam refocused on what he was doing. He flicked the whip again, a little harder, its tip catching Rae's clit. She screamed, her fingers curling into fists.

"Breathe," he reminded her. "Flow with the pain. Embrace it. Let it take you where you need to go."

She drew in a deep breath, her fingers loosening. He struck her again on her sensitive labia. She jerked and gasped. She was breathing hard, her eyes squeezed shut.

He waited.

Finally, she opened her eyes, which glittered in the candlelight. As he watched, she lifted her pelvis, arching forward, offering herself to his whip.

"Please, Sir," she begged. "Please."

Pride and lust surged through Sam in equal measure. He knew he would spend the rest of his life making himself worthy of her sweet submission. Aware she needed him to continue, he whipped her cunt, her inner thighs, her belly, her breasts, and then worked his way down again.

"Yes!" she cried over and over. "Again! Again! Please, Sir. Again!"

He didn't stop until she was crying, tears flowing down her cheeks, her body covered in a sheen of sweat. When he gauged she'd had enough, he dropped the whip and released her tethered ankles. Kneeling between her legs, he ran his hands lightly down her flanks and massaged her feet. Leaning over her, he released her wrists and rubbed her arms. She lay still, her hair tousled, her eyes fever-bright.

Her skin was marked with dozens of little welts he'd raised with his whip. Her cunt was dark red and swollen, its heady scent intoxicating. Crouching down, he licked the salty-sweet folds of her pussy, soothing away the sting of his lash. He placed a hand on either thigh, holding her open as he gently lapped at her labia, his tongue teasing over her clit.

He didn't stop until she was again begging, this time for permission to come.

"Not yet," he said at first, relishing his power, thrilled with her submission as he felt her struggle to obey. Reaching for his cock, he massaged it a moment, feeling it swell to full hardness, the tip gooey with pre-come. He maneuvered himself so he was ready, at the last second, to plunge into her heat.

He grunted with pure animal pleasure as he thrust inside her. It felt so fucking good—the fit between them better than perfect.

"Now!" he demanded. "Come for me *now.*"

He felt the delicious clench of her muscles against his cock as she spasmed and jerked beneath him. She wrapped her legs around his hips, pulling him in deeper as she came. Her arms encircled him, holding him with surprising strength as she undulated beneath him.

He pulled her up into his arms, covering her face in kisses as he thrust inside her, tumbling headlong into a climax as she held him close, locked in her tight embrace.

They lay still for a long while after, entangled in each other's arms. Sam felt something tear in his heart, a sweet wrenching pain. He understood Rae was in fact the one who wielded the real power, even if she didn't know it. She held his heart in her hands. It was at once frightening and exciting to realize his own vulnerability.

"Rae?"

"Hmm?"

"Who do you belong to?"

"You, Sir."

"And who do I belong to?"

"Me, Sir."

Also Available at Romance Unbound Publishing (http://romanceunbound.com)

Slave Island
Alternative Treatment
Switch
Dream Master
The Cowboy Poet
Safe in His Arms
Heart of Submission
The Solitary Knights of Pelham Bay – The Series
Texas Surrender
Unleashed Magic
Sarah's Awakening
Wicked Hearts
Submission Times Two
Confessions of a Submissive
A Princely Gift
Accidental Slave
Slave Girl
Lara's Submission
Slave Jade
Obsession: Girl Abducted
Golden Angel: Unwilling Sex Slave
The Toy

Frog: A Tale of Sexual Torture

Connect with Claire
Website: http://clairethompson.net
Romance Unbound Publishing:
http://romanceunbound.com
Claire's Blog:
http://clairethompsonauthor.blogspot.com
Twitter: http://twitter.com/CThompsonAuthor
Facebook:
http://www.facebook.com/s.php?init=q&q=clairethompsonauthor&ref=ts

Made in the USA
Lexington, KY
28 June 2012